Richard Gordon was born in 1921. He qualified as a doctor and then went on to work as an anaesthetist at St Bartholomew's Hospital, and then as a ship's surgeon. As obituary-writer for the *British Medical Journal*, he was inspired to take up writing full-time and he left medical practice in 1952 to embark on his 'Doctor' series. This proved incredibly successful and was subsequently adapted into a long-running television series.

Richard Gordon has produced numerous novels and writings, all characterised by his comic tone and remarkable powers of observation. His *Great Medical Mysteries* and *Great Medical Discoveries* concern the stranger aspects of the medical profession whilst his *The Private Life of...* series takes a deeper look at individual figures within their specific medical and historical setting. Although an incredibly versatile writer, he will, however, probably always be best-known for his creation of the hilarious 'Doctor' series.

The Captain's Table
Doctor and Son
Doctor at Large
Doctor at Sea
Doctor in Love
Doctor in the House
Doctor in the Nest
Doctor in the Nude
Doctor in the Soup
Doctor in the Swim
Doctor on the Ball
Doctor on the Boil
Doctor on the Brain
Doctor on the Job
Doctor on Toast
Doctors' Daughters
Dr Gordon's Casebook
The Facemaker
Good Neighbours
Great Medical Disasters
Great Medical Mysteries
Happy Families
The Invisible Victory
Love and Sir Lancelot
Nuts in May
The Private Life of Dr Crippen
The Private Life of Florence Nightingale
The Private Life of Jack the Ripper
The Summer of Sir Lancelot
Surgeon at Arms

Doctor in Clover

Richard Gordon

HOUSE OF
STRATUS

This edition published in 2001 by House of Stratus, an imprint of
Stratus Books Ltd., 21 Beeching Park, Kelly Bray,
Cornwall, PL17 8QS, UK.
www.houseofstratus.com

Typeset, printed and bound by House of Stratus.

A catalogue record for this book is available from the British Library
and the Library of Congress.

ISBN 1-84232-497-7

1

'You may be surprised to hear,' I announced to my cousin, Mr Miles Grimsdyke, FRCS, 'that I've decided to do the decent thing and settle down in general practice.'

'Do I attribute this decision to a severer sense of professional duty or to a severer hangover than usual?'

'Neither. But all my chums from St Swithin's seem to be installing wives and families and washing machines, and it seems high time I did the same. Take my old friend Simon Sparrow, for instance. Why, in the days of our youth we got chucked out of pubs together, and now his idea of whooping it up on a Saturday night is taking the lawn-mower to pieces. Believe me, I'm going to become dear old Dr Grimsdyke, the chap who's brought half the district into the world and pushed the other half out of it, beloved by all until it's time to collect old-age pension and chiming clock from grateful patients.'

'I suppose you realize, Gaston, how difficult it is these days to get into general practice?'

'Of course. Quite as bad as getting into the Test Matches. But not for fellows like me who know the ropes. You've heard of Palethorpe and Wedderburn, the medical employment agents?'

Miles frowned. 'The people in Drury Lane? I have never had recourse to them myself.'

'I happen to know old Palethorpe personally. We met last summer, on an occasion when I was able to offer him valuable professional advice.'

I didn't mention to my cousin we'd run into each other at Sandown Park races, where I put Palethorpe on such a good thing he'd kept my medical career close at heart ever since. Unfortunately, Miles has no sense of humour. It's the tragedy of modern life that so many people – dictators, tax collectors, tennis champions, teddy boys, and so on – seem to have no sense of humour, either.

'If you really intend to settle down,' my cousin continued, 'I might say I am delighted that you have chosen this particular moment to do so. In fact, I will confess that is exactly why I invited you for lunch today. More greens? One should keep up one's vitamin C this time of the year.'

'Enough is enough, thank you.'

It was one of those beastly days in midwinter when dusk chases dawn briskly across the London roof-tops, and fog was hazing even the chilly halls of the Parthenon Club where we sat. The Parthenon in St James's struck me as about as comfortable for lunching in as the main booking-hall at Euston Station, but Miles was one of the newest members and as proud of the place as if it were the House of Lords. I supposed it fitted into his self-portrait of the up-and-coming young surgeon. He was a small, bristly chap, generally regarded as embodying the brains of the family, who had just reached that delicate stage in a surgical career when your car is large enough to excite the confidence of your patients but not the envy of your colleagues.

'And how exactly are you earning your living at this moment?' Miles went on.

'I have many irons in the fire,' I told him. 'Though I must confess the fire isn't too hot. There's my medical articles for the popular press, to start with.'

Miles frowned again. 'I can't say I've noticed any.'

'They're all signed "By A Harley Street Specialist". Of course, it would be gross professional misconduct to put my own name.'

'You certainly show a remarkable ingenuity for practising without actually doing any medicine.'

'Which just proves what I've always held – medicine's a jolly good general education. It teaches you the working of everything from human nature to sewage farms. Not to mention all those little bits of Latin and Greek which are so useful in the crosswords.'

'But you must realize, Gaston, the time has come to put this free-and-easy existence behind you for good. You're not a mountebank of an undergraduate any more. You must now maintain the dignity of a qualified practitioner.

'Oh, I agree with you. Being a medical student is really the worst possible training for becoming a doctor.'

Miles dropped his voice below the hushed whisper permissible for conversation in the Parthenon.

'I am now going to tell you something in the strictest confidence.'

'Oh, yes?'

'Mr Sharper at St Swithin's is to become Professor of Surgery at Calgary University.'

'Really? I hope he enjoys crawling about in the snow potting all those bears.'

'That isn't the point. There will therefore be an unexpected vacancy on the surgical consultant staff. I shall in due course be applying for it. As Mr Sharper's own senior registrar, I do not flatter myself in believing my chances are excellent.' He helped himself to another boiled potato. 'Though as you know, considerations other than the strictly surgical sometimes weigh strongly with the selection committee.'

I nodded. 'I remember one chap was turned down because he wore knickerbockers and arrived for the interview on a motor-bike.'

'Quite so. To be perfectly frank, Gaston, it might embarrass me if you simply continued to flit about the medical scene – '

'My dear old lad!' I hadn't realized this worried him sufficiently to stand me a lunch. 'I may be a poor risk for a five-bob loan, but you can always rely on me to help a kinsman. A couple of weeks to say farewell to the haunts of my misspent youth, and I'll have made myself scarce from London for good.'

Miles still looked doubtful.

'I hope the permanency of your new position is more durable than some of your others.'

'They were mere flirtations with work. This is the real thing. And everyone will say, "See how that steady chap Miles has put even old Gaston Grimsdyke on his feet." '

'If that is indeed so, I'm much indebted to you. We may not always have seen eye to eye, Gaston – '

'Oh, come. Every family has its little misunderstandings.'

'But I assure you I have always acted entirely for your own good. And what precisely is this position you have in mind?'

'GP up north,' I explained.

I had been in Palethorpe's office that morning, when he'd greeted me with the news:

'I have exactly the right opening for you, Dr Grimsdyke. General practice in the Midlands – the backbone of England, you know. Assistant wanted, with a view, as we say. Start end of January. Dr Wattle of Porterhampton. A very fine man.'

'It doesn't matter what the doctor's like,' I told him. 'How about his wife?'

Palethorpe chuckled. 'How I wish our other clients were half as perspicacious! Fortunately, Mrs Wattle accompanied the doctor when he called, and I can assure you that she is a highly respectable and motherly middle-aged lady.'

'Nubile daughters?'

'It is their sorrow to be a childless couple, alas. I believe that is why they particularly asked me to find some decent, honest, upright, well-mannered, single young practitioner to share their home with them.'

'I can only hope you come as a nice surprise,' muttered my cousin when I told him.

'At last I feel set for a peaceful and prosperous career,' I went on, enlarging on my prospects a little. 'Who knows what the future holds? The dear old Wattles might take me to their bosoms. They might look upon me as a son to enlighten their declining years. They might send for their solicitors and start altering their wills. There should be plenty of lolly about in Porterhampton, too. They make turbines or something equally expensive up there.'

'My dear Gaston! You know, you really must grow out of this habit of counting your chickens before the hen's even ovulated.'

'What's wrong with a little imagination?' I protested. 'Lord Lister and Alexander Fleming wouldn't have got far without it. Anyway, at the moment roots are fairly sprouting from my feet like spring carrots.'

2

Until then Porterhampton was just another entry in my football pools, but a fortnight later I found myself driving past the Town Hall on a morning as crisp as an icicle, and pretty solemn I felt about it, too.

While lunching with Miles, I'd been putting an optimistic face on a pretty desperate situation, which is another of the useful things you learn from studying medicine. I didn't really like the prospect of being a respectable provincial doctor. In fact I didn't really like the prospect of being a doctor at all.

I was a *médecin malgré lui*. I'd taken up the profession because nobody in the family ever had the originality to think of anything else, and anyway all my uncles and cousins seemed to have a pleasant time of it, with large cars and everyone listening to their opinions at cocktail parties. But with medicine and marriage, the earlier you go in for either the riskier the project becomes. Quite a different chap emerges at the end of the course from the apple-cheeked lad with big ideas who went in. It's great fun at first, of course, being casualty houseman in a clean white coat with all the nurses saying 'Good morning, doctor,' even if the job does consist mostly of inspecting unpleasant things brought along in little white enamel bowls. It's a bit of a shock finding afterwards that you've got to make a living at it, though I suspect a good many housemen feel the same and keep pretty quiet. The public doesn't much care for entrusting their lives to doctors who don't love their profession, even though they entrust them every day to bus drivers and no one expects a bus driver to love his bus.

But as I couldn't go exploring like Dr Livingstone, become a Prime Minister of France like Dr Clemenceau, or play cricket like Dr W G Grace, I had to find a steady job like everyone else. And what of these Wattles? I wondered, as I drove past the Porterhampton fish market. They might at that moment be hopping about like a small boy waiting for the postman on his birthday. Or they might be plotting to kick me about like a medical tweeny. Fortunately for my low psychological state, I was soon reassured over my conditions of work.

I found the Wattles' house somewhere on the far outskirts, in a road of roomy Victorian villas apparently reserved for prosperous turbine-makers. As I drew up in the 1930 Bentley, the motherly Mrs Wattle herself appeared at the gate.

'Dear Dr Grimsdyke!' she greeted me. 'We're so delighted you've decided to bury yourself in our rather sleepy little town.'

'Charming place, I'm sure.'

'Mr Palethorpe spoke so highly of you, you know. I'm awfully glad he persuaded you to come. But you must be tired after your long drive. I'll show you to your room, and there's a nice lunch ready as soon as my husband gets in from his rounds.'

I slipped off my overcoat.

'Dear, dear! No buttons on your shirt, Doctor! You must let me have it tonight. And any socks and things that need darning, just leave them on the kitchen table.'

My room ran a bit to chintz and water-colours of St Ives, but seemed very cosy. There was a bookcase full of detective stories, a desk, and a large double bed already airing with a hot-water bottle like an old-fashioned ginger-beer jar. Going downstairs after tidying up, I found roast beef and Yorkshire on the table, with apple pie and Stilton waiting on the sideboard.

'I'm sure you'd care for a bottle of beer today,' cooed Mrs Wattle. 'Mr Palethorpe said you took the occasional glass.'

I'd met Dr Wattle himself only for a brief interview in London, and he was a little pink, perspiring chap with a bald head, resembling a freshly-boiled egg.

'Delighted to see you, my dear doctor.' He shook hands warmly. 'We may call you Gaston, may we? I hope you'll be very happy with us. Is that your car outside? Very dashing of you to drive an old open tourer. But do take my wife's Morris when it's raining, won't you? Would you care for an advance of salary? We'll sort out your duties later. If you ever want time off for anything, don't hesitate to ask.'

'Your chair's over here, Gaston. Sure you're not in a draught?'

'I hope you'll find my wife's cooking to your taste.'

'The roast beef's not overdone?'

'Anything special you fancy to eat, do please let us know.'

'Horseradish?' asked Mrs Wattle.

Later we had crumpets for tea and finnan haddock for supper, and in the evening we all three sat round the fire making light conversation.

'Mr Palethorpe revealed you had quite a roguish wit,' said Mrs Wattle, playfully shaking her finger.

So I told them the story about the bishop and the parrot, though of course altering the anatomical details a bit.

'How pleasant to hear a young voice in the house,' murmured her husband.

'We've so missed company in the evenings!'

'Ever since the dog died,' agreed Dr Wattle.

After years of living on tins of baked beans and packets of potato crisps, and mending my own socks by pulling a purse string suture round the hiatus, it did my physiology no end of good to have regular meals and all the buttons on my shirts. There wasn't even much work to do, old Wattle himself handling all the posher patients and leaving me with a succession of kids in the usual epidemic of mumps. After surgery and supper we all three gathered for the evening in the sitting-room. Sometimes we watched the telly. Sometimes we played three-handed whist. Sometimes they asked me to tell the story of the bishop and the parrot all over again. I was glad to see the Wattles had quite a sense of humour.

But even the Prodigal Son, once they'd used up all the fatted calf, must have hankered to waste just a bit more of his substance on riotous living. As the local amenities ran largely to municipal parks and museums, and so on, and as I couldn't go to any of the pubs because I was a respectable

GP, or to any of the pictures because I'd seen them all months ago in the West End, I longed for one final glimpse of the lively lights of London.

'Dr Wattle,' I announced one morning, when I'd been enjoying three square meals a day for several weeks. 'I wonder whether you'd mind if I popped down to Town this Saturday? I've just remembered I've got some laundry to collect.'

'My dear boy! Go whenever and wherever you wish.'

'That's jolly civil of you. Awfully annoying, and all that, but I'd better make the trip.'

The following Saturday evening found me once again in the genial glow of Piccadilly Circus, breathing the carcinogenic hydrocarbons and watching the neon sunrise as the lights came on.

I don't think there's any sensation to compare with arriving in London after a spell of exile, even if it's only your summer holidays. I felt I'd never seen anything so beautiful as the submarine glow of the misty street-lamps, heard anything as cheerful as the nightly torrent ebbing towards the suburbs, nor smelt any perfume so sweet as the reek of a London Transport omnibus. But I couldn't waste time admiring the scenery, and went to a telephone box, looked through my little black book, then rang up Petunia Bancroft.

Petunia was a little brunette and an actress. I've had a weakness for the stage ever since I was a medical student and nearly eloped with a young woman who was sawn in two twice nightly by a Palladium conjurer, until I discovered that she was in fact a pair of young women, and I'd picked the half with the shocking varicose veins. Petunia had been a chum of mine for many years, though unfortunately her ideas of entertainment rather exceeded her theatrical standing – usually she just walked on the stage and announced dinner was ready, but after the show she knocked back champagne like the great leading ladies when the stuff was five bob a bottle. Also, she had a rather hysterical personality, and was likely to throw the dessert about and bite the head waiter. But after a month in Porterhampton, Petunia seemed just what I needed.

'Darling, I'd love to meet you', she agreed. 'Don't come to the show, it's lousy and closing any minute, anyway. See you at the stage door after ten.'

The London streets were as deserted as Porterhampton on a Sunday afternoon by the time I took Petunia home to Balham — like most glamorous hotsies these days, she lived quietly with Mum and did the washing-up before catching the bus to the theatre. We'd had a pleasant little evening, what with supper and a night-club, and even if it did demolish Dr Wattle's advance of salary I was feeling like a sailor after ninety days at sea.

'Lovely time, darling,' said Petunia at the garden gate. 'When are you coming to live in London again?'

'One day, perhaps. When I retire.'

'When you retire! But darling, I won't ever recognize you then.'

'I'll have a chiming clock under my arm,' I told her. 'Night-night.'

The next morning I made my way back to the provinces for good, having wrapped all the Sunday newspapers in a large brown-paper parcel which I labelled THE EVERCLEEN LAUNDRY WASHES WHITER.

This little jaunt of mine was a mistake.

One taste of Metropolitan delights had ruined my appetite for Porterhampton for good. I'd tried really hard to fool myself I could merge with the local landscape. Now I realized I couldn't be comfortable anywhere in the world outside Harrods' free delivery area. I faced endless evenings watching the television and talking to the Wattles, and that night the prospect of both made me feel rather sickly over supper. But I had to stay in the place until the St Swithin's committee had shaken my cousin by the hand and told him where to hang his umbrella, and anyway the dear old couple were so terribly decent I'd never have forgiven myself for hurting their feelings over it.

'Dr Wattle,' I began, when we were alone after the meal. 'I don't know if I've told you before, but I've decided to work for a higher medical degree. I hope you'll not think me rude if I go to my room in the evenings and open the books?'

He laid a hand on my arm.

'I am delighted, dear boy. Delighted that — unlike so many young men these days, inside and out of our profession — you should take a serious view of your work.'

There was a catch in his voice.

'We are all mortal, Gaston,' he went on. 'In another few years I may no longer be here – '

'Oh, come, come! The prime of life – '

'And I should like you to be well qualified when you eventually take over this practice. My wife and I have become very attached to you these few short weeks. As you know, we have no children of our own. As a young man I suffered a severe attack of mumps – '

'Jolly hard luck,' I sympathized.

The mump virus, of course, can wreck your endocrine glands if you're unlucky enough to get the full-blown complications.

'If all goes well,' he ended, 'I hope you will inherit more from me than merely my work. I will detain you no longer from your studies.'

The rest of the week I sat in my room reading detective stories, and pretty beastly I felt about it, too.

Then one morning Mrs Wattle stopped me outside the surgery door.

'Gaston, my husband and I had a little chat about you last night.'

'Oh, yes?'

'We fear that you must find it rather dull in Porterhampton.'

'Not at all,' I replied, wondering if some revelling turbine-maker had spotted me in that night-club. 'There's always something happening,' I told her. 'The Assizes last week, the anti-litter campaign this.'

'I mean socially. Why, you never met any young people at all.'

It hadn't occurred to me that in Porterhampton there were any.

'So next Saturday evening I've arranged a little party for you. I do hope you can spare the time from your studies?'

Naturally, I said I should be delighted, though spending the rest of the week steeling myself for the sort of celebration to make a curate's birthday look like a night out in Tangier. When Saturday came I put on my best suit and waited for the guests among the claret cup and sandwiches, determined to make the evening a success for the dear old couple's sake. I would be heartily chummy all round, and ask the local lads intelligent questions about how you made turbines.

'Here's the first arrival,' announced Mrs Wattle. 'Miss Carmichael.'

She introduced a short girl in a pink dress.

'And here come Miss Symes and Miss Patcham.'

I shook hands politely.

'With Miss Hodder and Miss Atkinson walking up the drive. That's everyone,' she explained. 'Gaston, do tell us your terribly amusing story about the clergyman and the parrot.'

It struck me as an odd gathering. But old Wattle handed out the drinks while I sat on the sofa and entertained the girls, and after a bit I quite warmed to it. I told them the other one about the old lady and the bus driver, and a few more that I hadn't picked up from the boys at St Swithin's, and they all laughed very prettily and asked me what it was like being a doctor. I was quite sorry when eventually midnight struck, and everyone seemed to think it time to close down.

'I'm sure Gaston would drop you at your homes in his remarkable car,' suggested Mrs Wattle.

With a good deal of giggling, I discarded girls at various respectable front doors in the district, until I was finally left with only one in the seat beside me.

'I'm afraid I live right on the other side of the town, Gaston.'

'The farther it is, the more I'm delighted,' I replied politely.

She was the Miss Atkinson, a little blonde who'd given the parrot story an encore.

'Quite an enchanting evening,' I murmured.

'But you were so terribly amusing! I always thought medicos such stodgy old things, even the young ones.'

I gave a little laugh.

'We doctors are only human, you know.'

'I'm so glad,' she said.

After leaving her at another respectable door, I hurried home for some sleep. Nothing takes it out of you quite so much as telling a lot of funny stories.

3

'I know you'll be pleased,' announced Mrs Wattle a few mornings later. 'I've asked little Avril Atkinson to supper.'

'Very pleased indeed,' I told her courteously.

The fact is, I'd have been pleased whoever they'd asked, even my cousin. By then I'd discovered the dear old Wattles were incapable of conversation about anything except happenings in Porterhampton, which if you hadn't lived in the place for thirty years was like trying to enjoy a play after arriving in the second interval. It did me no end of good to hear another voice at table, even if they did make me tell the story of the ruddy parrot from the beginning.

After the meal I announced that my studies could slide for another evening, and politely joined the company in the sitting-room. Then Dr Wattle suddenly remembered he had a patient to see, and Ma Wattle had the washing-up to do, leaving Avril and me on the sofa alone.

'How about the television?' I suggested, Avril's conversation being almost as strait-jacketed as the Wattles'.

'Oh, let's. It's my favourite programme tonight.'

I switched on the set, turned down the lights, and when we'd watched a few parlour games and chaps pretending to get fierce with each other over the political situation, I very civilly drove her home.

'Do you like classical music, Gaston?' asked Mrs Wattle a few mornings later.

'I'm not adverse to a basinful of Beethoven from time to time,' I admitted.

'I'm so pleased. I've got a ticket for our little amateur orchestra next Friday in the Town Hall. Would you care to go?'

I was glad of an excuse to go out in the evening, now being rather bored with all those stories about chaps killing other chaps by highly complicated means. As I sat down among the potted municipal palms, I found Avril in the next seat.

'Quite a coincidence,' I remarked.

She smiled.

'You have such a sense of humour, Gaston. Wasn't it nice of Mrs Wattle to give us the tickets?'

'Oh, yes, quite.'

The dear old thing seemed to be getting forgetful, which I put down to the normal hormonal changes in a woman of her age.

The next few days were brightened by excitement over the great event in professional circles at Porterhampton, the annual medical dinner. As the Wattles seemed to find this a combination of the Chelsea Arts Ball and the Lord Mayor's Banquet, to please the dear old couple I agreed to put on a dinner jacket and accompany them, though personally nothing depresses me quite so much as a lot of other doctors. I had just eased into my chair in the ballroom of the Commercial Hotel, when I realized that I was once more sitting next to Avril Atkinson.

'So nice of Dr Wattle to have invited me,' she began. 'Are you going to make a speech with your terribly funny stories?'

'Not for me, I'm afraid. Though the fat chap with the microphone has a wad of papers in his pocket the size of an auctioneer's catalogue. Remarkable, isn't it, how men find so much to say after dinner when their wives haven't had a word out of them for years over breakfast?'

She giggled. 'Gaston, you're terribly witty.'

'Just wait till you've heard the fat chap.'

The guest on my other side having nothing to talk about except the progress of his patients and his putting, I passed the meal chatting lightly to Avril and when the floods of oratory had subsided took her home in my car.

'You simply must come in and meet daddy,' she invited.

Her father was a decent old boy, who gave me a whisky and soda and seemed intelligently interested in the National Health Service – rates of pay, prospects of promotion for young practitioners, and so on. I put him right on a few points, and went home with the pleasant feeling that I'd done my social duty by the dear old Wattles pretty thoroughly.

I suppose I'm a trusting sort of soul. Strangers at race meetings sell me useless tips at a quid a go. Motorists miss me by inches on zebra crossings. I cash dud cheques for fellows I meet in pubs. Small boys have me in knots on April the first. But it was probably the soporific effect of life in Porterhampton which delayed tumbling to my plight until the morning I was called to treat the girl with the pink dress from my party for mumps.

'When's it to be announced?' asked this Miss Carmichael, as I removed the thermometer from her mouth.

'What announced?'

'Don't play the innocent, Doctor. Everyone in Porterhampton has known about it for weeks. Your engagement to Avril Atkinson, of course.'

'Avril Atkinson!'

I picked up the bits of shattered thermometer from the floor.

'But dash it, that's ridiculous! I hardly know the girl.'

'Now, now! You're always being seen together, at concerts and dinners and things. As for the time she went to the Wattles' for supper – phew! She told me all about it. Sitting alone all evening on the sofa in the dark.'

I drove straight home and confronted Ma Wattle.

'So Dame Rumour hath been at work,' she said coyly. 'I am delighted, Gaston, for your sake. You see, my husband and I felt we were selfish monopolizing your cheery company. Now you're settling down here, it's only right and proper you should take unto yourself a wife. Unlike us, your later years will be comforted with sons and daughters, whom we shall look upon almost as our own grandchildren. I'm afraid I've rather been playing the matchmaker. But I'm so glad you chose Avril. Such a jolly girl! The pair of you are ideally suited.'

I had nothing to say. I went to my room. I paced up and down and glared at St Ives. I sat on the double bed and bit my nails. I wished I'd taken the advice of the Dean at St Swithin's and made my career in the Prison Medical Service.

I certainly didn't want to pass the rest of my life in Porterhampton, even if old Wattle bequeathed me the Town Hall as well. I certainly didn't want to marry Avril Atkinson, who'd probably make me tell the story of the parrot every morning over breakfast. Now I couldn't see how to avoid either. I've often read in psychology books about the acute anxiety state, but I never really understood it until then. Then I had one of those masterly ideas that sometimes come before the bell rings at the end of examinations.

'Mrs Wattle – Dr Wattle.' I appeared downstairs to find both of them in the sitting-room. 'I have something very painful to confess.'

They looked alarmed.

'I am already married.'

I felt this was the simplest way out. It was beyond me to tell the dear old couple that their own idea of my spouse was as ridiculous as picking the Matron of St Swithin's. With a bit of luck they'd kick me out on the spot, and possibly use up Avril on my replacement.

'My wife works in London. She is a nurse. A night nurse. I couldn't reveal her before, because…because the position which I have the honour to hold was advertised for a single man. I needed the work.'

I sounded so pathetic, I felt quite sorry for myself.

'If you will give me a few minutes to pack,' I ended solemnly, 'I shall remove my unworthy self from your lives for ever.'

'How unreasonable I've been!' cried Mrs Wattle, and burst into tears.

'We've deliberately set asunder two who have been joined together,' added Dr Wattle, beating his bald head.

'You must ask your wife to come at once, Gaston.'

'I'll double your salary.'

'We'll give you the run of the house till you find a place of your own.'

'All this might be rather inconvenient,' I interjected quickly. 'My wife's working every night. Important private case.'

'Then bring her for the day,' insisted Mrs Wattle. 'How about lunch on Saturday?'

'Yes,' agreed Dr Wattle, 'We shall be terribly upset if you don't.'

I felt the script had somehow got out of hand. Perhaps it might have been easier simply to have married Avril.

4

The following Saturday morning the Wattles' house was twittering with expectation.

'I'd better be off,' I announced, as the roast pork and stuffing sizzled in the oven. 'Her train's due in twenty minutes.'

'Do greet her with these chrysanthemums, Gaston.' Mrs Wattle pushed a bunch the size of a sheaf of corn into my arms. 'They're fresh out of the greenhouse, and I'm sure she'll love them. And I'm quite sure we're both simply going to *adore* her.'

I parked the car in the station yard, bought a platform ticket, and thoughtfully munched a bar of chocolate from a machine. I sat on a bench and read the paper until the train arrived. Peering through the passengers, I soon spotted the familiar red hat.

'Hello!' I called. 'Hope you didn't have a beastly journey.'

'It was stinking.'

'Welcome to Porterhampton.'

'And what a dump, too!'

'The city has several charming features, I assure you. Though I shan't be able to provide much of a conducted tour, as your train home's at nine-ten.'

'Thank God for that. What on earth have you got in your arms?'

'They're chrysanthemums, from the greenhouse.'

'You look as though you've lost your street barrow.'

'I think we'd better get off the platform. I might be spotted by one of my patients.'

I led Petunia Bancroft to the car.

'I've had some pretty funny parts in my time,' Petunia complained as we drove away. 'But this one makes the Crazy Gang look like the Old Vic.'

'It's perfectly simple,' I reassured her. 'You've only to play The Doctor's Wife, straight. To an accomplished actress like you, Pet my dear, it's as easy as selling theatre programmes.'

'If I hadn't been out of work I wouldn't have sniffed twice at the idea, believe you me.'

'Regard it as a professional challenge.'

'Costume all right?'

'Perfect for the part.'

'I thought I'd better leave off my ankle bracelet.'

'Can't say I've seen a nurse wearing one.'

'Supposing this old fellow – what's his name? – asks a lot of questions with long medical words and that? What the hell am I supposed to say?'

'Leave it to me. Anyway, all he's likely to talk about is our epidemic of mumps. Just remember the time you had it yourself.'

'I haven't.'

'Neither have I. Good job, in your case,' I smiled. 'Might possibly have mucked up your hormones.'

She asked how, so I gave a brief dissertation on the pathology and virology of mumps until we arrived at the Wattles' front gate.

'Petunia,' I announced. 'Your cue.'

I was pretty worried about the performance, though I didn't let on to Petunia. Another of the useful things you learn from studying medicine is radiating cheerful confidence all round while wondering what the devil's going to happen next. But I must say, she created the part of Mrs Grimsdyke magnificently. In half an hour the old couple were all over her.

'Where did you train, my dear?' asked Dr Wattle, as we sat down to lunch.

'Oh, at RADA,' said Petunia.

He looked puzzled. 'That seems a hospital I haven't heard of.'

'An affectionate name for the Royal Diabetic,' I told him.

'Is it really? Dear me, I never knew. One learns something every day.

And what is the trouble with this important case your husband tells us you're nursing?'

'Er – foot and mouth disease.'

'Attacking a human? Good gracious me! How extraordinary. I've never heard of such a thing before in my life.'

'Petunia means the poor fellow is down in the mouth because he's got one foot in the grave. Quite a common nurses' expression.'

'Is it indeed? Of course, you've had more recent contact with such things than I, Gaston. How one hates to be thought behind the times! I must try it out at the next BMA meeting. I expect, my dear, you've had wide experience nursing cases of mumps?'

But I neatly managed to steer the conversation away from shop, and as the afternoon wore on I felt my troubles were sorting themselves out splendidly. The old couple's feelings were saved, I was out of the matrimonial target area, and I could make a leisurely exit from Porterhampton as soon as Miles was safely on the St Swithin's staff. Besides, I now had a handy excuse for nipping down to London any weekend I felt like it.

'My train goes in about an hour,' Petunia reminded me, when we'd reached the cold ham supper stage.

'What a shame you can't stay longer,' sighed Mrs Wattle.

'Petunia has to be on duty at midnight,' I explained. 'As a matter of fact, I might as well be getting the car out.'

I opened the front door, and a nasty complication to my little plan rolled all over me.

I suppose this country wouldn't be the same if it weren't dosed regularly through the winter with fog. Can you imagine such national heroes as Sherlock Holmes or Jack the Ripper prowling about on nice mild summer evenings? How would Dickens' characters have looked in the Neapolitan sunlight? Or the dear old Houses of Parliament shining like the Taj Mahal? Our national character gets regularly tested by the frightful complications of fogs, particularly the great big grey thing that rose like a wall of dirty muslin from the front doorstep.

'I'd better telephone British Railways,' I muttered.

The word 'trains' evoked only a mystified silence on the wire,

'The midday hasn't turned up yet from Manchester,' said the fellow at the station. 'And where the morning express from Glasgow's got to, nobody knows. If you want your prospects of getting to London tonight, sir, they're nil. It's the biggest and thickest we've had this century, according to the wireless.'

'So now Petunia will have to stay till morning,' said Ma Wattle, smiling benevolently.

'But that's impossible!' she cried.

'Has to be back to her case,' I explained quickly.

'Surely under such circumstances a replacement could be found in London?' insisted Dr Wattle.

Petunia stamped her foot. 'Gaston can drive me.'

'Only into the first ditch, I'm afraid.'

'I absolutely and positively – '

I managed to shut Petunia up, the Wattles clearly thinking this rather odd behaviour for a pair of lovebirds.

'Don't worry, my dearest,' I pretended to give her a tender kiss. 'Leave it to me.' I hissed in her ear. 'I'll get you out of it,'

'I'm not worrying at all, my sweet. You'd blasted well better,' she hissed back.

We all sat down and looked at the television.

I spent the rest of the evening trying to concoct some fog-proof excuse. Should I pretend to perforate a duodenal ulcer? Or set light to the house? Or simply make a clean breast of it on the hearth-rug? I rejected each one. They would all upset the Wattles too much.

In short, nothing I could evolve by ten-thirty prevented the pair of us being ushered by Ma Wattle into my room, with two hot-water bottles in the double bed. 'You dirty little stinker!' started Petunia, as soon as the door was shut. 'This is the meanest and nastiest trick – !'

'For Lord's sake don't make so much noise! We're supposed to be a devoted couple.'

'I'd like you to understand, Dr Grimsdyke, that I am most definitely not that sort of a girl – '

'I know, I know! But if you'll only give me a moment's peace I can sort the whole thing out. No one is sorrier than I – '

'Nobody will be, by the time my brothers hear about this.'

'I can't help the ruddy fog, can I? Anyone would think I'd put it there myself.'

Petunia threw herself on the bed and started pounding the eiderdown. 'You've got to get me out of here! At once, I tell you. In five minutes. Otherwise I'll smash the window and scream for the police.'

'Pet, I'm doing my best! There must be some way of – '

'I'll scream. I will. I'll wake all the neighbours. You just listen – '

She drew a deep breath.

'For God's sake, Pet – !'

The telephone rang in the hall.

'Hold off the sound effects till I've answered it,' I hissed.

'Dr Grimsdyke?' said a woman's voice on the line.

'Speaking.'

'You swine! You cad! You beast! You bigamist!'

'Now just a second. If you'll tell me who's speaking – ?'

'You know perfectly well who's speaking. Avril, of course. I'm only ringing to inform you that tomorrow morning I'm starting a breach of promise suit, that'll blow you out of Porterhampton so hard you won't stop till you reach the white cliffs of Dover, which I hope you'll drop over and break your filthy neck. Let me tell you – '

'But I can explain absolutely everything,' I insisted. 'Can't I come round in the morning and see you?'

'You most certainly can't come anywhere near me. Apart from everything else I'm in bed with mumps, which I caught at your beastly party. *And* I've changed my cards to another doctor. You just wait till my brother comes on leave from the Commandos. Good night!'

In the space of five minutes I'd been abused by two women and threatened with assault from their relatives, which I felt was a record even for chaps like Bluebeard. But the telephone had given me an idea.

I tapped on the Wattles' door.

'I've been called to a case,' I explained. 'I don't expect I'll be long.'

Wrapping a scarf round my neck and pocketing a tin of cough lozenges from the surgery, I set out to spend the night in the fog while Petunia tucked herself cosily into the double bed.

5

The fog was lifting as I tramped back to the Wattles' home. I'd coughed my way into the darkness, with no particular object except keeping alive till morning. About a hundred yards from the house I'd wandered into the main road to London, where I met a chap who'd lost his lorry. He remembered a place in the area called Clem's Caff, which we found by walking an hour or so along the white line. The Caff sported a coke stove, and was full of lorry drivers in steaming overcoats, resembling overworked horses. I bought a cup of tea, which seemed to entitle me to sleep on the table like everyone else. About five-thirty I woke up, feeling as if I'd just been released from the rack in the Tower.

I crept inside the house, tapped softly at the bedroom door, and Petunia let me in.

'You look as if you've just come off Everest,' she said.

'I hope you passed a good night yourself,' I replied shortly.

'Absolutely adorable. I haven't been so warm for months.' She was already up and dressed, and seemed more amenable than the evening before.

'Poor Gaston! Are you sure you won't catch your death?'

'I wouldn't really care at the moment if I did.'

'I'm sorry – but it wasn't really my fault, was it? Perhaps you could have slept on the floor behind the wardrobe, or something.'

'I think it was a far, far better thing that I did.'

'You know, there really is something of the Sidney Carton about you, dear. No other man I know would have been half so noble.'

'Anyway, it's all over now. The fog's thinning rapidly, and as far as I remember there's a good train about five on Sunday afternoons. If you can stick it out till then.'

'I'm sure I can,' said Petunia. 'It's really awfully cosy here.'

'You *do* look pale this morning,' giggled Mrs Wattle when I appeared at breakfast. 'I hope you got plenty of sleep.'

The day passed without mishap. Petunia seemed quite to enjoy herself sitting about the house reading magazines, and in the afternoon I drove her to see the Town Hall, the waterworks, the bus depot, and the new abattoir.

'Quite a pretty little place after all,' she remarked, as I pulled up outside the municipal baths. 'It's a wonder I've never been here on tour.'

'Would you like to see the statue of the first Mayor?'

'Yes, please,' said Petunia.

After tea and Dundee cake I looked at my watch and announced to the Wattles, 'Perhaps my wife ought to be getting ready. We're due at the station in half an hour.'

'But isn't there a later train, darling?' asked Petunia. 'I could always catch that.'

'There's the eight forty-two,' I told her, looking surprised. 'And the ten six.'

'I'll take the ten six.'

'A far better idea,' agreed Ma Wattle. 'A few more hours together mean so much at your age, don't they?'

Shortly afterwards we were left alone. As a matter of fact, we were always being left alone, and Dr Wattle must have got awfully tired of sitting in his cold consulting-room.

'What's the idea, Petunia?' I demanded at once. 'I thought you couldn't get out of the place quick enough.'

She helped herself to a cigarette from the silver box.

'Gaston,' she said. 'I've been thinking.'

I flicked the Wattles' table lighter.

'Thinking what?'

'That this is the nicest part I've ever played.'

'You were a great success at it, thank you very much. And now for the final curtain.'

'But do you know *why* I was a success? I've just realized it myself. It was because I *felt* the part – here.'

She indicated her mid-sternal region.

'That's essential for all high-class acting, so they tell me.'

Petunia sat on the sofa.

'Do you remember, Gaston, what you told me in that night-club, the last time we were out together?'

Remembering what chaps tell them in night-clubs is another illustration of how women are congenitally defective in sportsmanship.

'That I was the dearest and sweetest girl you'd ever met, and how you wished you could live in my arms for ever?'

'Ah, yes.'

'Perhaps, Gaston, dear, you didn't think I took your remarks seriously?'

'Of course I did.'

As far as I remembered, she was hitting someone on the head with a balloon at the time.

'It's terrible how I have to disguise my feelings, my sweet. We actresses must always put our career first. We can never enjoy the simple home life of other women. It's awfully tragic.'

'I think you're perfectly right,' I told her briskly. 'Wonderful thing, devotion to one's vocation. You'll never regret it once you're a famous star with half London at your feet.'

'I'd never be a famous star. Not someone like Monica Fairchild, with every manager in London fighting over her. It's no good fooling myself. I'd just continue with walking-on parts, and live with Mum year in and year out, except for a few weeks on tour in miserable theatrical boarding-houses.'

'Oh, come! You're just a bit depressive for the moment. I bet Sarah Bernhardt felt exactly the same dozens of times.'

'But seeing you here,' Petunia went on, flicking her ash over the bearskin rug, 'in your dear little home in this sweet little town, has opened my eyes. My racket isn't worth the candle. I want to settle down.'

'But this isn't my dear little home,' I argued. 'It's Dr Wattle's dear little home. As for the town, I came here intending to settle for life and now I wouldn't even touch it for bed and breakfast. It would send a girl like you crackers in less than – '

She got up and stood so near me I could see the arteries in her conjunctivae.

'This last twenty-four hours I've realized how wonderful it is being your wife – '

'But dash it! You're *not* my – '

'You're so sweet, so modest. So honourable, so upright. So tender, so considerate, Gaston, darling, I've decided to accept you. We can get married secretly in some registry office – '

'Sorry to disturb the nest of lovebirds,' Ma Wattle chuckled, entering at that moment, 'I just wondered if your wife would like some nice hot soup for supper, to brace her for her journey.'

'Mrs Wattle.' Petunia turned to face her. 'I'm not going. I must stay with my husband. I'll send a telegram to London and resign my job. My mother can send on my things tomorrow.'

'I'm absolutely delighted!' exclaimed the old dear, embracing us. 'As I always say, a woman's place is at her husband's side, come what may. Of course, my children, you may stay with us as long as you wish. I'll just put the kettle on for your hot-water bottles. I expect after such excitements you'll both be wanting to go early to bed.'

If I wasn't keen on marrying Avril, I'd rather have swallowed the entire poisons cupboard before marrying Petunia. An agreeable companion for a gay night out, certainly. But you can't make a life partner of a woman who keeps trying to conduct the band with sticks of celery.

'You haven't eaten your nice soup, Gaston,' said Ma Wattle at supper.

'Not very hungry, I'm afraid.'

'What a wonderful thing love is!'

I was nearly sick over the sliced brawn.

I was edgy and jumpy the rest of the evening, which, of course, the idiotic Wattles put down to passion, or the expectation thereof. Worst of all, the mental trauma of the past two days seemed to have beaten my brain into paralysis. Nothing I could contrive by ten o'clock prevented Petunia and myself again being shown into my bedroom.

'Alone at last!' breathed Petunia.

'Yes, but only for a couple of shakes,' I told her smartly. 'As soon as the Wattles have bedded down, I'm going to skip it into the night again.'

'But Gaston! Surely you're not going to leave your wife?'

'Pet, you chump! You're not my wife – only on the programme. Let me make it perfectly clear I'm not going to stay with you up here.'

'How honourable you are!' she breathed. 'How fine! How different!'

The Grimsdykes, of course, have their honour. But I must admit I wouldn't have objected to the same arrangement if we'd been in a hotel at Brighton instead of the Wattles' spare bedroom. Under prevailing circumstances the only place for me was Clem's Gaff.

'We'll be married tomorrow if you like,' she said, starting to unzip her dress. 'A girl friend of mine once got a special licence terribly easily.'

'Petunia! You don't understand – '

'I understand everything, darling. You're a wonderfully honest man, and I shall love you more and more as the years go by.'

About twenty minutes later I was sitting again over one of Clem's cups of tea. I woke at five-thirty the next morning, so ill from the effects of prolonged exposure that I would almost have married Petunia on the spot for a comfortable night's rest in my own bed. I got back to the house shivering and with a shocking headache, and found Dr Wattle in the hall.

'Just come in from seeing the Mayor's gout,' he greeted me. 'I didn't know you'd been called out too. I never heard the phone.'

'It was someone with fits. Difficult diagnosis. Took a lot of time.'

'You don't look very perky, my boy. Are you sure you're all right?'

'Bit chilly, this night air.'

'Perhaps I'd better take your temperature?'

As he removed the thermometer from my mouth he asked, 'Ever had mumps? Well. I'm afraid you have now.'

'Mumps!' I cried. 'But – but that means isolation.'

'I'm afraid so. You'll have to stay in your room. Your wife hasn't had it either? Then you'd better be strictly alone. I'll go up and break the sad news. It's best for you not to breathe over the poor child.'

'Petunia's rather alarmed about it,' explained Dr Wattle, returning with some surprise. 'She seemed remarkably upset over those hormonal complications. I told her how terribly rare they are, but she's still awfully agitated. Keeps saying it would ruin her career. I shouldn't have thought it would have mattered much one way or another to a nurse. However, it's none of my business. We'll make you up a bed in the attic.'

I slept for twenty-four hours, which Dr Wattle later wrote a letter about to the *BMJ* entitled 'Unusual Stupor in Epidemic Parotitis'. Petunia spent the morning gargling, then disappeared for London. As soon as my lumps were down I announced I must go to the sea-side for convalescence, and sent a wire from London explaining I'd been summoned to a dying uncle in South Africa.

I felt pretty sorry for myself. I'd broken a couple of girlish hearts, had a nasty illness, and expected hourly to be assaulted by Commandos, and so on, in the street. Porterhampton had thenceforward to be blotted from my atlas. And now I had to explain it all to my cousin.

But at least I never hurt the dear old Wattles' feelings.

6

'From your appearance,' started Miles, 'you would seem to have finished some protracted party.'

'If you must know,' I replied, rather hurt, 'I've had a nasty attack of epidemic parotitis. I've hardly got over it yet.'

'I'm sorry.'

It being one of my principles always to confess my short-comings promptly, particularly if they're likely to be discovered pretty quickly anyway, I'd telephoned Miles on arrival and invited myself to dinner. I now sat in his South Kensington drawing-room wondering how best to explain the retreat from Porterhampton.

'And when are you returning to your practice?' asked Miles.

I shifted on the sofa.

'As a matter of fact, old lad, I'm not.'

'What? Damn it! You've not been thrown out already?'

'Thrown out?' I looked offended. 'I resigned, with the dignity of a high-principled Cabinet Minister.'

Miles fell silent. To fill the gap I reached for a magazine – one of the shiny ones which report the activities of all our best-bred young women and horses.

'That's what I need,' I said, indicating a photograph of people with long drinks on a yacht at Cannes. 'A few weeks in the sunshine to buck me up.'

Miles made a noise like a tearing sheet of canvas.

'Damnation, Gaston! Are you mad? Are you fit for some institution? Here you are – out of work, penniless, a walking disgrace to your family if not to your entire profession, and you ramble about weeks in the sunshine. Really!'

I tossed the magazine aside with a sigh.

'The trouble is, you're perfectly right,' I admitted. 'I'm not the shining figure of the eager young doctor.'

'You're the shining figure of the shiftless young wastrel, and I don't mind telling you. I seriously advise you to see a psychiatrist. He might at least be able to explain your highly unstable occupational history.'

'The fact is, old lad, I don't need a psychiatrist to tell me that I don't like medicine very much.'

Miles stared as though I were Cinderella telling the Fairy Godmother she didn't care greatly for dancing.

'At Porterhampton the dear old couple handed me every chance to settle down as a respectable family man and family doctor. But do I want to be the modern GP, signing certificates for all the uninteresting patients and hospital letters for all the interesting ones? No, I jolly well don't. And neither do a lot of other chaps, judging by the correspondence in the *BMJ*. As I'll never be a specialist in anything, and I couldn't possibly sit in the Town Hall with a map of the local sewers doing public health, there isn't much left. The trouble is, I'm temperamentally unsuited to my work.'

'But think of all those years of study – wasted!'

'They're not wasted a bit,' I argued. 'Look at all the famous chaps who've benefited from a medical education – Leonardo da Vinci, John Keats, Chekhov, and so on. Not to mention Crippen.'

'You must quite definitely see a psychiatrist. And meanwhile, how precisely are you going to earn your bread?'

'Ah, yes. I agree, that's the problem.'

Further discussion about my professional future was prevented by the appearance of Miles' wife.

'How charming you're back so soon, Gaston,' she greeted me. 'We quite thought you'd gone to seek your fortune up North.'

'I decided that opportunity taps less faintly in London, Connie.'

'I'm so glad. Now we'll see much more of you. What did you say, Miles, dear?'

'Nothing, nothing,' muttered Miles.

I knew Connie pretty well. In fact, once I was in love with her.

This happened when I was a student and Miles had just qualified as Mr Sharper's junior casualty house-surgeon, and pretty pleased with himself he felt about it, too. As I reflected during dinner that evening, Miles and I had never really hit it off at St Swithin's, or even as kids. Miles was the one who didn't get his boots dirty, always had his sums right, wasn't sick at all the parties. and didn't make a fuss about his tonsilectomy. At school he used to make me blow up his football and toast his crumpets. Then I followed him to St Swithin's, and like everyone else started medicine by dissecting the dogfish, which has put me off fish suppers ever since. Miles was already well into the course, and by the time I got as far as the anatomy rooms kept buttonholing me in the corridors with fatherly advice.

'If you spent a little more time dissecting and a little less writing all those stupid jokes for the students' magazine,' was his usual line, 'you might show you were taking your career seriously.'

'I thought the last one was rather funny. About the girl who said she suffered from claustrophobia because she had a terrible fear of confinement.'

'Take it from me, Gaston, you'll regret this frivolity one day. You stick to your anatomy. It's the grammar of medicine.'

'Personally.' I disagreed, 'I think they only fill medical students with anatomy like they used to fill kids with brimstone and treacle. The experience is obviously so unpleasant, everybody agrees it must be doing them good.'

'I'm not at all certain it isn't my duty to write to my father,' he generally ended.

My own father having unfortunately perished in the RAMC, I was brought up under a Victorian system of guardians, with Dr Rudolph Grimsdyke as chief paymaster. Uncle Rudolph practising at the time out East, Miles was his nark on the spot, and I suppose he sneaked in the end because half-way through the course the old boy cut my allowance by half. I know that ever since *La Bohème* it's been thought rather romantic for students to starve in garrets holding the tiny frozen hands of their girl-friends, but that sort of existence didn't appeal to me at all. Particularly as all the girls I knew seemed to complain shockingly of the draughts even in comfortable cocktail bars.

Shortly after the onset of this financial anaemia Miles qualified, glittering with scholarships and prizes.

'Gaston,' he said, getting me into a corner of the St Swithin's Casualty Department one winter afternoon, 'I want a serious word with you.'

'Oh, yes?'

'I'd be much obliged if you'd try to embarrass me a little less now that I'm on the St Swithin's junior staff. You must realize that I, at least, don't wish the entire family to be made ridiculous throughout the hospital. It's bad enough your always disappearing to the dog-races, but this habit of taking menial employment – '

'My dear old lad, I assure you I don't do it for fun. Anyway, it's all your old man's fault, being so tight-fisted. Surely you know by now I dislike work in any form whatever?

I was at the time restoring my enfeebled exchequer with such casual jobs as dish-washing in West End restaurants and bar-keeping in East End pubs, and had just finished a profitable though strictly limited run as Father Christmas in an Oxford Street store.

'That's not the point at all. Mr Sharper was certain he saw you the other day. He was extremely blunt to me about it this morning.'

'Oh, really? I thought his keen surgical eye had pierced the whiskers. But I bet he only made a fuss because I told his beastly kids to ask for a complete set of electric trains and a couple of motor-cars.'

'I do wish you'd take this seriously, Gaston!'

'Let's talk about it another time. I must be off now, I'm afraid. Otherwise I'll be late for work.'

A few days after this argument I met Connie, by accident. All medical students dream of witnessing some really satisfactory road smash, then appearing on the scene to calm the panic-stricken bystanders with the magic words, 'I am a doctor.' I've done it myself three times. The first, the policeman told me to run home to mother. The second, I grabbed a tourniquet from some fumbling old boy and discovered he was the Professor of Surgery at St Asaph's. Now, of course, I walk rapidly in the opposite direction and leave it to the ambulance boys, remembering Sir Lancelot Spratt's resuscitation lecture – 'When I chuck myself into the Thames in despair, ladies and gentlemen, I hope I'll be given artificial respiration by a fit Boy Scout, and not some middle-aged medical practitioner who's soon more out of breath than I am.' But when one is young, one doesn't consider such things. On this third occasion, as soon as I heard the scream of brakes and tinkling of glass, I leapt into the middle of Sloane Square and took sole charge.

In the next part of the dream, the injured party isn't a poor young child or a dear old lady, but a beautiful girl having hysterics. And that's exactly what I found. So I popped her in a taxi and drove her round to the casualty entrance at St Swithin's, where Miles organized X-rays, diagnosed a Colles' fracture. and signed an admission form for his ward.

'Charming girl, too,' I observed, as Connie was wheeled away.

'Thank you, Gaston, for holding the X-rays.'

'Always glad to help. I might pop up and see her later. Terribly important to follow-up cases, so they keep telling us.'

'Mr Sharper allows only his own students in his wards, I'm afraid.'

'Oh, come. Can't you stretch a point?'

'A point, being defined as possessing position but not magnitude, is incapable of being stretched,' said Miles.

All the same, I went up the next morning with a bunch of roses.

'How terribly sweet!' exclaimed Connie, looking beautiful despite the plaster and bandages. 'And your assistant's just called too, with the mimosa.'

'Assistant?'

'The doctor who helped you with the X-rays.'

'Ah, yes. Useful chap.'

The staff in modern hospitals outnumbering the patients by about five to one, the inmates can be excused for confusing the ranks. I remembered there was once a frightful row when Sir Lancelot Spratt in a white coat was mistaken for the ward barber.

'You'll be out of here this afternoon,' I went on, not bothering to start long explanations. 'When time has healed all your wounds, would you care to come out for a bite of dinner?'

'But I'd love to, Doctor!'

'Jolly good. I'll get your telephone number from the ward notes.'

Unfortunately, Connie turned out to be the daughter of a shockingly rich fellow from Lloyd's, so I couldn't buy her a pint of beer and show her the ducks in St James's Park and pretend I'd given her an exciting evening.

Also, I knew a determined chap like Miles wouldn't easily give up. While I was sitting with her a few weeks later in the Savoy, hoping she wouldn't feel like another drink, I remarked casually, 'Seeing much of my cousin these days?'

'As a matter of fact, yes. I'm going to the theatre with him tomorrow.'

'It may be rather cheek of me to ask this, Connie, but I'd rather you didn't mention me to him, if you wouldn't mind.'

She looked surprised. 'Why ever not?'

'Just to save the poor chap's feelings. These little family jealousies, you know. He feels it rather, being my underling at the hospital.'

'How awfully considerate of you, Gaston. Naturally, I won't say a word. But supposing he talks about you?'

'He never does,' I assured her. 'Another Martini?'

'Yes, please,' said Connie.

I passed a couple of enjoyable months escorting Connie to all the more fashionable plays and restaurants, particularly as she still seemed to imagine that I was some wealthy young specialist, and I never seemed to find the chance to put her right. Then one afternoon Miles cornered me in the surgeons' room.

'I believe you've still been seeing Connie?' he demanded.

I tossed my sterile gown into the students' linen bin.

'On and off, yes.'

'I'd like you to know that I – I'm perfectly serious about her.'

This didn't disturb me. Miles was perfectly serious about everything.

'May the best man win, and all that, eh?'

'Damn it, Gaston! I wish you wouldn't regard this as some sort of sporting contest. I happen to love Connie deeply. I wish to make her my wife.'

'Good Lord! Do you really?'

The notion of Miles making anyone his wife seemed as odd as palm trees growing on an iceberg.

'And I'll thank you not to trifle with her affections,' he added.

'You will, will you?' I returned, feeling annoyed at his tone. 'And how do you know I don't want to make her Mrs Grimsdyke, too?'

'You? You're in no more position to marry than a fourth-form schoolboy.'

I felt the conversation was becoming embarrassing, and edged away. Besides, I had to be off to work again.

Entertaining Connie was making such inroads into my finances that I'd been obliged to find more regular employment. Fortunately, I'd met a chap called Pedro in a Shaftesbury Avenue pub, and after giving him some free advice about his duodenal ulcer and a good thing for Kempton Park, I was offered five evenings a week as a waiter in his Soho restaurant. Pedro was a fierce task-master, most of his relatives still chasing each other over Sicilian mountains with shotguns, and I had to clean all the soup off my best set of tails every night before going to bed, but the tips were good enough compensation for both.

Or they were until that particular evening, when Miles walked in with Connie.

'Shall we sit over here?' she said, advancing towards my corner. 'I hate a table too near the door.'

I ducked quickly into the kitchen.

'What the 'ell are you up to?' demanded Pedro.

'I – er, just wanted to adjust my sock suspenders.'

'I don't pay you to adjust your socks, mister. You get back in there. There's customers just come in.'

I passed a hand across my forehead.

'You know, Pedro, I don't think I'm feeling very well tonight. A bit faint. I might be sick over the fish or something. If you don't mind, I'll just totter through the staff entrance and make home to bed.'

' 'Ow the 'ell you think I run my business one man short?' Pedro picked up a carving knife. 'You leave this restaurant only over your dead body, see mister? If you want to be sick, come out and be sick in the kitchen, like everybody else. You go to work.'

I edged back through the swing doors. I slipped my menu and table-napkin behind a bread basket, and prepared to dash for the pavement. I'd almost made the main entrance, when Connie glanced idly round and spotted me.

'Why, it's Gaston! Hello, there! You dining here, too?'

Miles turned round and scowled.

'Oh, hello, Connie. Yes, I am, as a matter of fact. Expecting an old school chum. Chap called Honeybank. Doesn't seem to have turned up.'

'Charming little restaurant, isn't it?'

'Oh, very.'

'You seem very dressed up,' muttered Miles.

'Going on, you know, A ball, and all that.'

'I think men look their best in tails,' remarked Connie. 'Don't you Miles? What on earth's dear Pedro doing?'

I thought dear Pedro was probably putting that knife on the grinding machine, but only murmured something about having to be off,

'But if you haven't eaten you must stay for a bite with us,' Connie insisted, 'I'm sure Miles wouldn't mind.'

'Not a bit,' growled Miles.

'It might be a little awkward, actually – '

'But definitely. Gaston. Tell the waiter to bring another chair. Ah, there you are, Pedro. How is your lovely *canneloni* tonight?'

'Delicious, madame.'

Pedro came over rubbing his hands. I stood on one foot, leaning against the table. Dashed difficult, striking an attitude simultaneously suggestive of helpful servility and longstanding chumminess.

'And the *osso buco*, it is excellent,' Pedro added,

'Then shall we all have *canneloni* followed by *osso buco*?' Connie looked inquiringly at Miles and myself. 'I'm terribly hungry.'

'Two *canneloni* two *osso buco*,' snapped Pedro in my ear. 'Didn't you 'ear what madame says?'

'How extraordinary repeating the order like that,' exclaimed Miles.

'Just a little joke,' I explained, as Pedro backed away. 'I know him very well.'

Connie sighed. 'How lucky you are! I can't imagine anything more useful in London than being friends with all the head waiters. But Gaston, *do* sit down. You make me feel uncomfortable, standing about like that.'

'Just a second, if you'll excuse me. Phone call – the school chum, you know.'

I slipped back to the kitchen.

'What the 'ell's the matter with you tonight?' demanded Pedro. 'You stick around with a silly grin on your face like a drunk monkey. How you expect me to run my restaurant if you don't listen to the customers?'

'Look, Pedro, I really think I ought to be at home tucked up in bed – '

'Take that in, and don' talk so much.'

He handed me two dishes of *canneloni*.

'Good Lord!' exclaimed Miles. 'You've brought the food yourself.'

'Ha ha! Just another little joke. Dear old Pedro, you know. I keep threatening a public health inspection of his kitchen, and just nipped in to take him by surprise. The canneloni was ready, so I brought it along.'

Connie found this terribly amusing.

'But Gaston, you haven't a plate. And do please sit down.'

'I'll just prop on the back of this chair.' I edged myself into a position where I might be mistaken for serving the spinach. 'They get so terribly crowded, I'm sure Pedro hasn't got a spare seat. I don't think I'll try any *canneloni* myself, thanks. But let me help you.'

'You serve quite professionally,' exclaimed Connie.

'Jack of all trades, you know...'

'Are you sure you're quite all right tonight?' demanded Miles.

'Oh, fine, thank you.'

I felt that the situation was reasonably hopeful, as long as they crammed down their blasted *canneloni* before Pedro came back.

'What were we talking about? I suppose you've heard the story of the bishop and the parrot – '

Just then a voice behind me called, 'Waiter!'

'Well, you see, this bishop had a parrot – '

'Waiter!'

'And this parrot used to belong to an old lady who bought it from a sailor – '

'Say, Waiter!'

'There isn't a waiter in sight,' interrupted Connie.

'Never is when you want one,' grumbled Miles.

'I think he's an American who keeps shouting,' said Connie.

'And the old lady always used to keep it under a green baize cloth in the front parlour. Every morning she'd take the cloth off the cage, and every morning the parrot said – '

'Hey, Waiter, for chrissakes!'

A fat man I'd just served with cigars and brandy appeared at my elbow.

'Excuse me, folks. I just wanted to tell the waiter here I've had a darned fine meal and darned fine service. I reckon it's the best I've struck since I've been in Europe. I was just getting on my way when I thought, shucks, I gotta give credit where credit is due. Thanks a lot, son. This is for you.'

The beastly chap stuffed a pound note into my top pocket.

'But how extraordinary,' exclaimed Miles.

'He thought you were the waiter!' laughed Connie.

'People never notice the fellows who serve them with food,' I mumbled. 'Conan Doyle or Edgar Wallace or someone wrote a story about it.'

'But he did seem pretty definite.' Miles gave me a nasty look.

'Oh, Miles, you know what Americans are,' said Connie. At that moment, Pedro appeared again. I pretended to be arranging the flower vase.

'Everything all ri'?'

'No,' said Miles. 'The waiter hasn't brought any grated parmesan with my *canneloni*.'

Pedro glared across the table.

'Zere is no grated cheese with the *canneloni*.'

I glanced round for the cheese thing. I might reach across for it with a little laugh.

'That's exactly what I said,' Miles returned. 'It happens that I'm particularly fond of grated cheese with my *canneloni*.'

'So am I,' said Connie.

'There is no grated cheese with the *canneloni*!' shouted Pedro in my direction.

'Good gracious, man!' exclaimed Miles. 'Don't yell at me like that.'

'I am *not* yelling at you like that, monsieur. I am yelling at '*im* like that. *There is no grated cheese on the canneloni!*'

Connie jumped up.

'How dare you address my guests in that manner! I am going to leave this restaurant this very instant.'

Pedro looked as if he'd been hit in the neck with one of his own *canneloni*. 'Guests, madame? What guests? You're fired,' he added to me.

'I shall never eat here again, and I shall tell all my friends not to eat here either. Come along, Miles. Treating our guest here as one of your waiters – '

But, damn it, madame! 'E *is* one of my waiters. 'E come every night, part time – '

'Only five days a week,' I insisted.

'Gaston!' Connie gave a little gasp. 'Is this really true?'

I nodded. The Grimsdyke ingenuity had been beaten back to its own goal-line. I reached for my napkin and automatically flicked the tablecloth.

'I'm not a doctor, really,' I murmured. 'I'm a student. I take this on for a little extra dibs.'

There was a silence. Connie started to laugh. In fact, she laughed so long she almost asphyxiated herself with a stick of Italian bread. In the end we all four thought it a tremendous joke, even Pedro.

But Connie never looked at me the same way again. And a fortnight later got engaged to Miles. I was pretty cut up about it at the time, I suppose. I often wonder how life would have turned out if Miles had been more of a gentleman and taken her somewhere like the Ritz.

The only compensation was that, according to the American chap, if I had to be a waiter I was a damn good one.

7

'I'm afraid I was somewhat over-optimistic at the way things would go at St Swithin's,' announced Miles.

Connie had left us after providing a charming little dinner, and I was guessing my chances of getting a cigar.

'The appointment of Sharper's successor has as usual got mixed up with hospital politics.'

He stared gloomily into the fruit bowl.

'Sir Lancelot Spratt is making an infernal nuisance of himself on the committee. He is opposing my candidature, purely because Mr Cambridge is supporting it. Sir Lancelot has quarrelled with him, you know. Cambridge refuses to knock down his old clinical laboratory, and Sir Lancelot wants to park his car there. To think! My future decided by a car park.'

'There's nothing like a mahogany table and a square of pink blotting-paper to bring out the worst in a chap's character,' I sympathized. 'How about the other runners?'

'There are thirty other prospective candidates for the post, all as well qualified as I. But we are mere pawns, mere cyphers. Perhaps I should apologize for being short with you earlier, Gaston. The strain, you know. The uncertainty...'

He miserably cracked a nut. I felt sorry for the chap. Personally, there was nothing I'd have liked less than being a consultant at St Swithin's, having to wear a stiff collar every day and never being able to date up the nurses, but it had been Miles' ambition ever since he was cutting up that dogfish. And I rather felt that Connie, too, fancied herself in a new hat running the hoop-la with other consultants' wives at the annual hospital fête. Besides, Miles was the brightest young surgeon St Swithin's had seen for years, and I should have felt a bit of a cad not helping so worthy a practitioner along the professional path.

'If you didn't get on at St Swithin's,' I tried to console him, 'you'd find a consultant job easily enough in the provinces.'

'But it wouldn't be the same thing. And, of course, Connie and I would have to leave our home.'

I nodded. Since the waiter episode girls had been in and out of my life like people viewing an unsatisfactory flat, but I'd always retained a soft spot for Connie. The thought of her confined for life to a place like Porterhampton upset me so much I'd almost have had another go at living there myself to prevent it.

'In such delicate circumstances,' I suggested, 'I take it you'd more than ever like me tucked away in some respectable job?'

'Exactly.'

'Find me one, old lad, and I will. I can't possibly face Palethorpe for months, of course.'

'I have some influence with the Free Teetotal Hospital at Tooting. They'll be needing a new house-surgeon next week.'

'And the week after, I'm afraid, as far as I'm concerned.'

Miles stroked his pale moustache.

'A pity you didn't keep your position on the *Medical Observer*. At least it utilized your talent for the pen respectably.

'That was a congenial job,' I agreed, 'until the old editor banished me to the obituaries.'

The *Medical Observer* was the trade press, which lands on doctors' doormats every Friday morning and is widely appreciated in the profession for lighting the Saturday fires. It has an upstairs office near the British Museum in imminent danger of condemnation by the health, fire, and town planning authorities, where I'd been assistant to the editor, a thin bird with a wing collar and severe views on the split infinitive.

'You can't imagine how depressing it was, writing up dead doctors from nine to five,' I told Miles. 'Though I composed my own for the files while I was there, and a jolly good one it will be, too. Yours isn't bad, either.'

'I am gratified to hear it. Perhaps you should go abroad? An oil company for which I do insurance examinations are prospecting up the River Amazon in Brazil. They have a vacancy for a medical officer on a five-year contract. The salary would certainly appeal to you. And you just said you could do with some sunshine.'

'But not five years of it, all at once.'

Miles began to look irritable again. 'I must say, Gaston, for a man in your position you're being extremely difficult to please.'

'Oh, I don't know. If I'm going to sell my soul I might as well get a decent price for it.'

'I do wish you'd discuss the subject of your livelihood seriously.

'I was just about to, old lad. I don't suppose you could advance me ten quid, could you? Resigning abruptly from Porterhampton left me a month's salary short.'

'You know I am against loans among relatives. But I will agree if you accede to my suggestion about the psychiatrist. I am certain that's what you need. I can easily arrange for you to see Dr Punce, who manages the aptitude tests for the oil company. He rather specializes in whittling down square pegs.'

I don't share the modern reverence for psychiatrists, mostly because all the ones I know are as cracked as a load of old flower-pots. But the financial blood was running so thinly I accepted.

'I suppose you have no serious plans at all for maintaining yourself?' Miles asked, putting away his cheque book.

'I've a few more medical articles on the stocks. I'd also thought of trying my hand at a bit of copywriting – you know, "Don't let your girdle be a hurdle, we make a snazzier brassière," and so on.'

Miles winced. 'Gaston looking for another job?' asked Connie, appearing with the coffee. 'That's no problem anyway. A bright young man like him should be in demand anywhere.'

A bit *infra dig*, I thought, a doctor going to a psychiatrist. Like a fireman ringing the station to say his house was alight. I didn't remember much of the psychiatry course at St Swithin's myself, except the afternoon Tony Benskin was left to hypnotize a young woman with headaches, and once he'd got her in the responsible state suggested she took her blouse off.

Apparently Tony's hypnotic powers are low voltage, because the girl clocked him one against the corner of the instrument cupboard. Quite some confusion it caused when the chief psychiatrist came in, to find the patient stamping about shouting and the doctor unconscious.

But I dutifully appeared at Dr Punce's rooms in Wimpole Street the following afternoon, and found him a tall, thin fellow in striped trousers, a pince-nez on a black ribbon, and side-whiskers. I was shown in by a blonde nurse, which put me in a awkward position at the start – if I gave her the usual once-over the psychiatrist might decide something pretty sinister, and on the other hand, if I didn't, he might decide something even worse. I hit on a compromise, and asked her what the time was.

I took a seat and prepared for him to dig into my subconscious, shaking the psychopathic worms out of every spadeful.

'I don't suppose you treat many doctors?' I began.

'I assure you that all professions are fully represented in my case-books.'

'Psychiatry is the spice of life, and all that?' I laughed.

But he had no sense of humour, either. 'The note I have from your cousin mentions your difficulty in finding congenial employment,' he went on, offering me a cigarette, as psychiatrists always do.

I nodded. 'Miles seems to think I should find a job with security. Though frankly I rather prefer insecurity. But I suppose that's a bit of a luxury these welfare days.'

'H'm. I am now going to recite a succession of words. I wish you to say the first word that comes into your head in reply. Light?'

'No, it's going very well, thank you. I've got some matches of my own.'

'That is the first word.'

'Oh, I see. Sorry. Yes, of course. Er – sun.'

'Night?'

'Club.'

'H'm. Sex?'

'Psychiatrists.'

'Line?'

'Sinker.'

'Straight?'

'Finishing.'

'Crooked?'

'Psychiatrists. I say, I'm terribly sorry. I didn't mean to say that at all.'

Dr Punce sat for a while with his eyes closed. I was wondering if he'd had a large lunch and dozed off, when he went on, 'Dr Grimsdyke, I have had a particularly heavy month with my practice. I fear that I am sometimes tempted to be rude to my more difficult patients.'

'If it's any consolation,' I sympathized with him, 'I'm tempted quite often too. But don't worry – the feeling will pass. I recommend a few days in the open air.'

'Have you heard the story of the donkey and the salt?' he asked bleakly.

'No, I don't think I have.' I settled down to listen, knowing that psychiatrists pick up quite a few good ones in the run of their work.

'I'd like you to follow it carefully. There was once a donkey who fell into the water, crossing a stream on a very hot day with a load of salt. Eventually he got to his feet, feeling greatly relieved because the water had dissolved his burden. The next day he was crossing the stream loaded with sponges. This time he deliberately fell, but the sponges soaked up so much water the donkey was unable to rise at all. The animal succumbed. What do you think of that?'

'Ha ha!' I said. 'Jolly funny.'

In fact, I thought it a pretty stupid story, but one has to be polite.

'You think that the story is funny?'

'Oh, yes. Best I've heard for weeks. I suppose you know the one about the bishop and the parrot?'

'Dear me, dear me,' said the psychiatrist, and started writing notes.

After a good many questions about the Grimsdyke childhood, which was just the same as any other beastly little boy's, he asked, 'Any sexual difficulties?'

'By Jove, yes.'

I told him the story of Avril Atkinson, but he didn't seem impressed.

'Your trouble, Dr Grimsdyke,' he finally decided, wiping his pince-nez, 'is that you find yourself in uncongenial employment.'

I asked him what I was supposed to do about it, but he only said something about it being a consulting-room and not the Labour Exchange.

'I mean, being a doctor doesn't train you for anything else much, does it? Not like some of those barristers, who get fed up standing on their feet drivelling away to judges and collect fat salaries running insurance companies.'

'There have been medical bishops and ambassadors. Rhodesia had a medical Prime Minister. Goethe and Schiller were, of course, once both medical students.'

'Yes, and Dr Gatling invented the machine gun, Dr Guillotin invented the guillotine and Dr Dover became a pirate. I don't think I've much qualification for any of those professions, I'm afraid.'

'I suggest some non-clinical branch. How about entymology? Are you fond of insects?'

I thought deeply. 'Well, if I'm really no good as a doctor I suppose I could always end up as a psychiatrist. I say, I'm terribly sorry,' I added. 'Just for the moment I was forgetting – '

'Good afternoon, Dr Grimsdyke.'

'Right-ho. Do you want to see me again?'

'No. I don't want to see you at all. The nurse will show you out.'

I left him shaking his head and fumbling nervously with his pince-nez. The poor chap looked as though he really ought to have seen a psychiatrist.

'How did you get on?' asked Connie, answering the door when I called to report.

'Well, I think I won.'

'I hope he recommended shock treatment. Your Uncle Rudolph's in the sitting-room.'

'Good Lord, is he really? Where's Miles?'

'Out on a case. But don't worry – Uncle only wants to offer you a job. One of those rich patients who've been buying up the local country houses has asked him to Jamaica for a holiday. As he's got twenty-four hours to find a locum for the next three months, I suggested you.'

'That's really very decent of you, Connie.'

Since returning from the East, the old uncle had settled at Long Wotton, a pleasant niche in the Cotswolds with thatched roofs and draught cider and cows in the High Street. My session with the psychiatrist not producing much alternative to a lifetime of GP, and Miles' ten quid already having undergone severe amputation, I felt glad of a decent job anywhere. I consoled myself that half rural practice is veterinary medicine anyway, and I'm rather fond of animals.

'My daughter-in-law talked to me for thirty minutes before persuading me to take you as my locum,' Uncle Rudolph greeted me. He was smaller and bristlier than Miles, with hair and eyebrows like steel wool under the influence of powerful magnets, and an equally prickly ginger tweed suit.

'That's very civil of you, uncle,' I told him, 'but as a matter of fact, you're not putting me to any trouble, as I'm quite free at the moment.'

'If you come to Long Wotton on Thursday, I can hand over. My Mrs Wilson will look after you adequately. Though she is attuned to the habits of an elderly widower, so don't expect champagne and caviar for breakfast.'

'Good Lord, no. I couldn't possibly manage anything heavier than cornflakes in the morning, anyway.'

'Kindly remember, Gaston, that there are a large number of important people in the neighbourhood. Most of them are my patients, and I wish them to remain so. Now listen to me. I understand from Miles that you are short of cash?'

'I am rather undernourished in the pocket at the moment,' I admitted.

'You know I have certain funds under my control which I saved you dissipating as a medical student. If you behave sensibly and efficiently at Long Wotton I am prepared to release them. If not, you will have to wait until my demise. And I can assure you that my blood-pressure is excellent.'

'All that matters, uncle,' I told him, 'is giving you satisfaction. In fact, you might just as well advance me the cash now.'

But he didn't scent to grasp the point, and hurriedly asked Connie to fetch him another whisky and soda. Shortly afterwards Miles came in, and nobody took much notice of me any more.

8

I arrived in the country on one of those April days when all the flowers look freshly painted and all the girls look beautiful. The English spring had arrived, as described in the poems and travel advertisements instead of the grey slushy thing we usually get.

I'd already spent a few week-ends at Long Wotton, and found it a friendly place where the inhabitants are all acquainted, if not, as I later suspected from the general feeble-mindedness, all actually related. Although I'm not much of a one for country pursuits – guns make such a frightful noise, fishing gives me a bad cold for weeks, and I regard horses as highly unroadworthy vehicles – it was pleasant to find myself respected locally as a learned chap, and not just the fellow who dishes out the chits for false teeth. Also, there was a very amiable young sub-postmistress, and I was looking forward to a few months quietly letting life go by and Avril Atkinson and Porterhampton fade into my subconscious.

After a week or so I was even becoming a little bored, with existence presenting no problems more complicated than keeping the uncle's housekeeper happy, and she seemed very satisfied with the story of the bishop and the parrot. Then I returned one evening from repairing the effects of a pitchfork on some bumpkin's left foot – a very pleasant consultation, with everyone touching their forelocks and asking if I could use a side of bacon – and found the old dear herself standing at the garden gate, looking distraught.

'Doctor, Doctor!' she called. 'Something terrible's happened.'

I was a bit alarmed the cream might have gone off. I was looking forward to my evening meal of fresh salmon followed by early strawberries, particularly as the old uncle had overlooked handing over the cellar keys in his hurry to be off, and I'd just found them – buried under the coal in the outhouse, of all places.

'Doctor, you're to go at once,' she went on. 'It's very urgent. To Nutbeam Hall,' she explained, when I asked where. 'It's his Lordship, there's been a terrible accident.'

A bit of a tragedy, I felt. Fancy missing a dinner like that. But the Grimsdykes never shirk their professional duty, and pausing only to load the Bentley with sufficient splints and morphine to tackle a train crash, I sped up the road to Nutbeam Hall.

Everyone in Long Wotton knew Lord Nutbeam, of course, though I don't mean they played darts with him every night in the local. In fact, most of the inhabitants had never seen him. The old boy was a bachelor, who lived in a rambling house apparently designed by Charles Addams, his younger brother's missus doing such things as ordering the coal and paying the milkman. He appeared only occasionally when they gave him an airing in an old Daimler like a mechanized glasshouse, always with brother or wife as bodyguard.

This was the pair who received me in the hall, a long, dim place crammed with furniture and as stuffy as the inside of the family vault.

'I'm the doctor,' I announced.

'But Dr Grimsdyke – ?'

'Dr Rudolph Grimsdyke is enjoying a little well-earned holiday. I'm his locum and nephew, Dr Gaston Grimsdyke.'

I saw them exchange glances. The Hon. Percy Nutbeam was a fat chap with a complexion like an old whisky-vat, which I suppose he'd acquired at his brother's expense. His wife was one of those sharp-faced little women with incisors like fangs, to whom I took an instant dislike.

'Of course, I'm perfectly well qualified,' I added, sensing they might not take kindly to anyone but the accredited family practitioner.

'Naturally, naturally,' agreed Percy Nutbeam, very sociably. 'We don't question that for a moment.'

'I am sure you've had very extensive experience, Doctor,' put in the wife.

'Well, very varied, anyway. Look here,' I told them, feeling rather awkward, 'unless it's a matter of saving life on the spot, if you'd rather call another practitioner – 'Not at all,' said Mrs Nutbeam briskly. 'My husband and I have the utmost confidence in your handling his Lordship's case. Haven't we, Percy?'

'Of course, Amanda.'

I must admit this made me feel pretty pleased. The old uncle's full of homely advice about wool next to the skin and so on, but after all those years among the hookworm and beriberi he's as out of date in medical practice as a Gladstone bag. I could see they were delighted at an up-to-date chap like myself with all the latest from hospital.

'Then what's the trouble?' I asked.

'We fear a broken hip, doctor,' announced Amanda Nutbeam. 'That's serious, I believe?'

'Could be. Very.'

'Our aunt died after a broken hip,' murmured Percy.

'It all depends on the constitution of the patient,' I told them, remembering my orthopaedic lectures.

'Please let me impress upon you, Doctor,' said Amanda, 'that his Lordship is very delicate.'

'Very delicate indeed,' added her husband. 'This way, Doctor, if you please.'

I went upstairs feeling pretty curious. I'd already decided it was the old story – poor old Lord Nutbeam was potty, and the family were making themselves thoroughly miserable keeping it quiet, instead of getting him decently certified and sending him baskets of fruit every Friday. I was therefore a bit startled when my clinical examination provided a couple of eye-openers.

In the first place, far from being dotty, Lord Nutbeam had an IQ in the professorial class.

'I fell from the library ladder, Doctor,' he explained from his bed. 'Appropriately enough, as I was reaching for my first edition of *Religio Medici*. You are familiar with the work? Perhaps you have also read Dr William Harvey's *De Motu Cordis* in the original Latin? I should much like to discuss it with a medical man.'

Not wishing to chat about all those books I'm going to read whenever I get a spare moment, I put my stethoscope in my ears. Then I got my second surprise. From the conversation downstairs I'd gathered Lord Nutbeam's grip on life was as secure as on a wet conger eel, but I quickly discovered – fractures apart – he was as hale and hearty as I was.

'I am very delicate, Doctor,' he kept on insisting, though he looked a spry old boy with his little white moustache. 'I neither smoke nor drink and live on soft foods. Ever since I had the fever at the age of twenty-one my dear brother and his wife have been devoted to my welfare.'

'Don't worry,' I told him. 'We'll soon have this little matter cleared up, and you'll be able to go on reading just where you left off.'

A few minutes later I again faced the ambulant members of the Nutbeam family in the hall, and announced in suitably sepulchral tones that his Lordship had indeed fractured the neck of the right femur.

'Ha!' muttered Percy Nutbeam, 'Auntie!'

'Then it *is* serious, Doctor?'

'But please let me reassure you.' I possibly gripped my lapels. 'Once we get anyone as chirpy as Lord Nutbeam into hospital and the hands of a decent orthopaedic surgeon, we'll have him on his feet again in no time. Meanwhile, I have administered a sedative and the fracture isn't very painful. I guarantee he'll stand up to everything wonderfully.'

I was then rather jolted to hear Amanda Nutbeam ask, 'Doctor, don't you think it would be far, far kinder just to do nothing?'

'A very eminent specialist left our aunt to pass peacefully away,' added Percy.

'But dash it!' I exclaimed. 'How old was your aunt?'

'Ninety-two.'

Lord Nutbeam was fifty, the age when most men are telling their secretaries they're in the prime of life.

'Look here, this is quite a different case – '

'His Lordship is so delicate, life is merely a burden to him,' persisted Amanda.

'Been delicate for years, Doctor. Even in the nursery he was always being sick.'

'Surely, Doctor, it would be a happy release?'

'He will have no more troubles among the angels,' ended Percy Nutbeam, looking at the chandelier.

Now, I may not be the most erudite of medical practitioners, but many years' patronage of the sport of kings has left me pretty sharp at spotting something fishy. So I eyed this couple pretty sternly and said, 'If I don't get Lord Nutbeam into hospital this very night, it'll be – why, gross professional misconduct, to say the least.'

'You can hardly get him there without his consent,' replied Amanda sharply.

She gave me a smile as unfriendly as one of Sir Lancelot Spratt's laparotomy incisions.

'And Lord Nutbeam would never consent to anything whatever without consulting us first,' said Percy.

'Now just a minute – '

'You are very young, Doctor,' Amanda continued. 'I can assure you his Lordship would be much happier passing away peacefully in his own home, rather than being mutilated among strangers.'

'Our aunt,' added Percy, 'was very contented right to the end.'

'Here, I say – '

'I think your consultation is over, Doctor. The butler will show you to the door.'

9

I was so furious I couldn't enjoy my salmon. But I managed to cram down the strawberries and a bottle of the uncle's *Liefraumilch*, then I paced the room and smoked a couple of his cigars. I looked up Watson-Jones' *Fractures and Joint Injuries*, and I found a copy of Hadfield's *Law and Ethics for Doctors*, but though this is pretty hot on such things as Relations with the Clergy and Opening a Vein after Death, it's a bit short on handling murderous relatives. I wondered what the devil to do. I thought of telephoning another doctor, but felt this would produce only an action for slander. Finally I decided (*a*) if old Nutbeam continued to lie flat on his back he would undoubtedly perish; (*b*) you can't press-gang people into hospital; and (*c*) some pretty nasty questions were going to be asked at the inquest.

Apart from medical ethics, the thought of the beastly brother and wife itching to get their fingers on Lord Nutbeam's cash and title fairly made my blood boil. Particularly as I now realized my welcome to Nutbeam Hall didn't come from heartfelt appreciation of my clinical abilities, but because they thought I had more chance of knocking his Lordship off than my uncle had. After sitting down with a drop of the uncle's special liqueur brandy, I made my decision. My only course, as a doctor and gentleman, was to return to Nutbeam Hall forthwith and give all concerned a jolly good piece of my mind.

Five minutes later I arrived again at the front gates, turning a few choice phrases over in my thoughts, when I noticed a ruddy great Rolls parked outside. I was wondering if the Nutbeams had simply preferred to by-pass me and summon a specialist off their own bat, when the front door opened to admit a severe-looking bird of consultoid aspect, wearing striped trousers and carrying a briefcase.

'Good evening, sir,' I said.

'Good evening,' he replied, got into his Rolls, and drove off.

I'd hardly time to sort this out when the door flew open again and Mrs Nutbeam fell on me like her long-lost baby.

'Doctor, Doctor! Thank God you've come hack! You must get his Lordship into hospital at once.'

"This very instant,' cried Percy, panting up behind.

'With the very best specialist available.'

'Regardless of expense.'

'Everything humanly possible must be done for him.'

'The telephone is just inside the hall, Doctor.'

'Now just a minute.' I found this rather confusing. 'A couple of hours ago you told me – '

'Please disregard whatever I said a couple of hours ago,' returned Amanda Nutbeam, 'I was too upset by my dear brother-in-law's accident to think properly.'

'We both were, Doctor. We were quite beside ourselves.'

Deciding there was no point in asking a lot of silly questions, I telephoned an eminent bone-basher in Gloucester who'd done a neat job on a patient who went through a threshing machine. Shortly afterwards I was gratified to see Lord Nutbeam departing tucked-up in an ambulance, particularly as the original Grimsdyke diagnosis had been confirmed.

Like any GP pushing his patient into hospital these days, I didn't see his Lordship again for a fortnight. I was meanwhile kept agreeably busy remedying the rustics, and though the uncle didn't even send a postcard, Miles telephoned a couple of times, but he was too concerned over Sir Lancelot's car park to ask how I was getting on. Then one Saturday I decided to drive over to Gloucester to watch an afternoon's cricket, and looked into the Jenner Memorial Hospital to see Lord Nutbeam during the tea interval.

I found his Lordship very perky in a private room with a Smith-Petersen pin holding his hip together, though we hadn't much time for a quiet chat – modern orthopaedic wards are pretty active places, with all those nice girls from the physiotherapy department laying cool hands on fevered joints and making you kick your legs in the air as though you were about to turn out for the Arsenal. But the old boy seemed to be enjoying it all, and while a little red-headed staff nurse brushed his hair he started asking my views on the original works of Hippocrates.

'You'll soon be back among your books again,' I said, not wishing to pursue the subject.

'Indeed, Doctor, I believe my library is the only pleasure in my life. Except on Saturday nights, when I sometimes play the piano.'

I was reflecting that this sort of existence would have me stone dead in a fortnight when we were interrupted by the surgeon himself, a big, red-faced, jolly Irishman. Most orthopods are, when you come to think of it, just as ophthalmologists look like dyspeptic watchmakers and bladder surgeons resemble prosperous commercial travellers.

'He's all yours now, m'boy,' said the surgeon, as we left the room together after examining the patient. 'His rehabilitation will go much smoother at home, and this sister-in-law seems agreeable enough to nurse him. Anyway, I'm off on Monday for a month's fishing in County Mayo. How is he for cash, by the by?'

'According to village gossip, crammed with it.'

'Is he now?' The orthopod seemed to brighten at the prospect of having his fishing on Lord Nutbeam's hip. 'Odd sort of feller, don't you think? I couldn't see him saying "Boo" to a newly hatched gosling. I'll be sending you the usual letter about treatment. Meanwhile, tell him to confine his reading to the bottom shelf.'

When a few mornings later they unloaded his Lordship at Nutbeam Hall and I pushed his new wheel-chair into the library, I felt pretty contented with myself. The whole episode had already increased my professional standing in Long Wotton no end. I'm far from saying the natives were hostile, but in the country they regard anyone who hasn't lived among them for thirty years as a day tripper, and now there was plenty of glowing gossip to warm the ears of the old uncle on his return. If I could present him with a Lord Nutbeam skipping about the front lawn, he'd not only give fewer of those old-fashioned looks whenever I suggested enterprising lines of treatment, but painlessly disgorge my cash on the spot.

'I am certainly glad my brother-in-law is back in his own home, Doctor,' remarked Amanda Nutbeam. 'It is only here, I think, that we really understand his best interests.'

'So I've noticed,' I told her. 'And now for a few weeks of rest and quiet and nourishing food,' I added confidently, 'and his Lordship will be dancing the Highland Fling if he wants to.'

But I should have learned long ago that in the turf and therapeutics it's disastrous to back a dead certainty.

For some reason, Lord Nutbeam didn't want to get better. I'd imagined that once he was home he'd settle down to a nice long read, but instead he sat staring out of time window with cups of beef-tea getting cold at his elbow. Sometimes he picked up *The Anatomy of Melancholy*, but it didn't seem to hold him. Sometimes he pushed himself to the piano, but he could manage only a few bars of *Valse Triste*. To cheer him up, I wheeled him round the garden telling funny stories, but he never seemed to see the point. 'Alas, poor Yorick!' was the most I could get out of him.

His Lordship grew steadily feebler and feebler, while everything else in sight was burgeoning wildly in the sunshine. It wasn't long before I began to grow alarmed about his condition. Modern medicine's all very well, with antibiotics and heart-lung machines and so on, but once a chap's decided he doesn't want to live any more we're not much better off than the witch-doctors in Central Africa. And my professional problems weren't made easier by the other Nutbeams, who now the excitement had died down treated me like the man come to mend the drains. Far from his Lordship, they were terrible snobs – particularly the missus, whom everyone knew in the village was only a road-house remnant from Percy Nutbeam's youth, anyway.

'It would be much more convenient if you could make your daily visit earlier,' she said, as I limped into Nutbeam Hall one evening after a heavy day's practice among the pig-sties. 'We are expecting Lord and Lady Farnborough for dinner any minute, and I should naturally prefer my guests not to be greeted in the hall by the doctor. Perhaps you would also have the goodness to change your shoes before coming to us, Dr

Grimsdyke. I realize that you cannot avoid walking through the farmyards during the day, but – '

I must say, her attitude made me pretty annoyed. Particularly as I felt she wouldn't have tried it with the old uncle, not with those old-fashioned looks of his. Then, a couple of days later, Lord Nutbeam went off his food and started looking like Socrates eyeing the hemlock.

'We're all bursting to see you back to normal again,' I told him, hopefully writing a prescription for another tonic. 'Here's something which will have you chirping with the birds in no time.'

'Thank you, Doctor. You are very kind. Indeed, everyone is very, very kind. Especially, of course, my dear brother and his wife.' He listlessly turned a few pages of Gibbon's *Decline and Fall*. 'But I fear my accident had more effect than I imagined. I've hardly been out of Nutbeam Hall for many years, you know, on account of my delicate health. Meeting so many people in the hospital was something of a disturbance. You are doubtless familiar with the lines in Gray's *Elegy in a Country Churchyard* – '

Feeling that churchyards were definitely out, I interrupted with the story about the parrot. But I don't think he got that one either.

I left him in the library, wondering whether to assemble the family again and confess the old boy wasn't living up to my prognosis. But I was stopped by Percy Nutbeam himself in the hall.

'Could you spare time for a whisky and soda, Doctor?'

My professional duties being over for the day, I accepted.

'I'm very worried about my brother's condition,' he declared, after a bit of chat about the weather and the crops.

'And so am I,' I told him,

'I remember the case of our aunt so well. The collapse seemed to set in all at once. Like a pricked balloon. I suppose there's not any danger of – er, is there?'

I nodded. 'I'm afraid I've got to say there is.'

The poor chap looked so concerned I felt I must have misjudged him all along.

'Then how long, Doctor, would you give him – ?'

'Might be a matter of only a week or two,' I said gloomily.

'Good God! Not before May the twenty-eighth?'

I looked puzzled, wondering if they'd arranged a picnic or something. 'This is a very delicate business, Doctor.' He poured himself another whisky. 'But I must be frank with you, You remember Sir Kenneth Cowberry ?'

'I don't think I've had the pleasure

'He was leaving as you returned, the night of the accident. He's the head of Hoskins, Harrison, Cowberry, and Blackthorn. My brother's accountants, you know. I thought we'd better send for him at once, in case there were any arrangements my brother might have wished – '

'Quite,' I said.

'Lord Nutbeam naturally desires to leave my wife and myself his entire fortune. After all, we have devoted our lives to his welfare.'

'Quite, quite.'

'But it was only that evening we learned – my brother is oddly secretive about money matters – that he had in fact already made over his estate to me. In order to – er, escape death duties. You may have heard of other cases, Doctor? But under the rules of the Inland Revenue Department my brother must stay alive for five years after signing the document, or it doesn't hold water. And those five years are up at midnight, May the twenty-eighth. So, Doctor, if you can keep him alive till then – I mean, I hope and trust he will have many happy years among us yet – you understand the position…?'

I didn't think highly before of this pint-sized Lord and Lady Macbeth. Now I felt it would serve them damn well right if the Government carted off the lot, to pay, among other things, my National Health salary.

'I understand the position very well,' I replied, wishing I could produce one of the uncle's looks.

I'd very much taken to old Nutbeam, and I was determined to keep him alive for the full three score and ten. But the situation was getting beyond a chap of my modest experience, and out in the country I hadn't any of my chums to ask for advice. I wished the uncle would get fed up sitting on the beach at Montego Bay and come home. I even wished Miles would turn up for the week-end. I was wondering what to say next when I had another of those profitable inspirations of mine.

'I think it would be wise,' I announced, 'to have another opinion. There might be some other condition I've overlooked. After all, doctors can make mistakes. Just like accountants.'

'As many opinions as you wish, Dr Grimsdyke.'

'There's a man in Harley Street just right for this type of case. Though his private fees are rather high.'

'That's of no concern at all, I assure you.'

'And, of course, he'll charge a guinea a mile for the visit.'

Percy Nutbeam looked a bit concerned doing the mental arithmetic, but he agreed, 'Nothing is too expensive with my brother's life at stake.'

'Plus his first-class fare and meals, naturally. He's a general surgeon, but I guarantee he's got the sharpest diagnostic nose in London. His name's Sir Lancelot Spratt.'

10

'Delightful air,' declared Sir Lancelot.

I'd driven over to Greater Wotton Junction to meet him, and pretty nervous I felt about it, too. In my days as a student at St Swithin's, Sir Lancelot and myself disagreed about everything from the way I tried to treat appendicitis to the way I tried to treat the nurses, and his last remark the day I proudly told him I'd qualified was that the Archbishop of Canterbury would presumably now have to make an addition to the Litany.

I bowed him from his carriage like royalty come to open the local fat stock show.

'I hope you've no objection to travelling all this way, sir?' I began, feeling that I'd sent for Rembrandt to paint the attic.

'Objections? Why, boy? It is the duty of consultant surgeons and the fire brigade to give their services whenever and wherever they are needed. It is, moreover, extremely pleasant to escape from London on a summer morning, and I'm being handsomely paid for it. Don't be so damned humble, Grimsdyke!' He poked me in the epigastrium with his walking-stick. 'A doctor must feel humble only towards his own abilities. Excellent roses, these. Apricot Queens, I believe? What sort of mulch d'you use?'

This remark was directed to the stationmaster, Greater Wotton being one of those junctions regarded as an exercise in landscape gardening interrupted by the occasional arrival of trains. Sir Lancelot then ignored me for ten minutes' erudite discussion on the merits of horse and cow manure. Come to think of it, that sort of ability represents his genius. Most surgeons can talk only about the inside of their patients or the inside of their cars, but Sir Lancelot has informed views on everything from nuclear physics to newts.

'I am presumably obliged to travel in that,' he said, indicating my car. 'Am I permitted a bite to eat before seeing the patient?'

'I've arranged a modest meal, sir.'

Remembering that a high blood-sugar is conducive to mental tranquillity, I'd decided to give the old boy a jolly good lunch before getting down to business.

'I rarely take wine at midday,' Sir Lancelot observed later, mellowing over the roast lamb and a glass of the uncle's Château Lafite, 'but I must say Dr Rudolph Grimsdyke has excellent taste in it.'

I agreed, though I'd been a bit alarmed to notice the cellar had somehow got down to only a couple of bottles.

'The only locums I did were in the East End of London, where in those days the doctors were as half-starved as the patients.' Sir Lancelot gazed through the window, where the cuckoos were tuning up among the blossoms. 'He seems to have found himself a very agreeable spot – botanically, ornithologically, and even meteorologically.'

'But not anthropologically, sir,' I said brightly, feeling it time to mention the Nutbeams,

'According to the essayist Hazlitt,' Sir Lancelot observed with a nod, 'all country people hate each other. You will now kindly recapitulate the family history of your patient. You were not particularly explicit on the telephone.'

An hour later the pair of us were marching into Nutbeam Hall,

I think the Hon. Percy and his repulsive missus were staggered to find themselves faced with a chap in a frock coat and a wing collar, who glanced round as though he'd been sent to condemn the place by the local Medical Officer of Health.

'We are delighted, Sir Lancelot,' simpered Amanda Nutbeam, who of course thought doctors were all right as long as they had titles. 'I am so pleased you accepted our invitation to take over his Lordship's case.'

Sir Lancelot looked as though she were a junior probationer who'd dropped a bedpan in the middle of his weekly ward round,

'Madam, I have *not* assumed clinical responsibility for Lord Nutbeam. His medical adviser remains Dr Gaston Grimsdyke, at whose invitation I stand here now.'

'Oh! Of course, Sir Lancelot – '

'That is normal professional procedure.'

These remarks put my morale up no end. Despite our differences in the past, Sir Lancelot wasn't so much offering the olive branch as proffering ruddy great groves. But I should have realized that a chap like him would back me to the scalpel hilt, now that I was qualified and one of the boys.

'We shall see the patient, if you please.' The Nutbeams looked rather flustered. 'And I should be glad if you would kindly provide me with a clean hand towel.'

I remembered Sir Lancelot always demanded a clean towel in uppish households, and in a tone inferring that it was a pretty stiff request.

'Dr Grimsdyke will lead the way,' he went on, as I stepped respectfully aside. 'The patient's doctor precedes the consultant into the sickroom. That is etiquette, and I should be the last to alter it.'

Our consultation was a great success. Sir Lancelot started by discussing ancient Chinese medicine for twenty minutes, then he examined the patient, had a chat about Byzantine architecture, and left his Lordship looking his brightest for weeks.

'And you discovered the original fracture solely from the physical signs, Grimsdyke?' he asked, as we left the room.

'Yes, sir.'

'Congratulations. The difficulty in making such a diagnosis is matched only by the disaster of missing it.'

'That's – that's very kind of you, sir.'

'I believe in giving credit where credit is due. In your case it happens to he remarkably easy.'

I felt jolly pleased with myself, all the same. Though I've always maintained that orthopaedic surgery is only a branch of carpentry, and now I come to think of it I was rather hot stuff in the woodwork class at school.

The other two Nutbeams were waiting expectantly in the hall, but at the foot of the stairs Sir Lancelot simply picked up his hat.

'Sir Lancelot – ?'

Percy looked as though this wasn't much of a run for their money.

'Yes, Mr Nutbeam ?'

'Have you – er, anything to say about my brother?'

'I shall have a consultation with my colleague here, who will inform you later. That is the normal procedure.'

'But if you could hold out even a word of hope – ' exclaimed Amanda, I fancy glancing stealthily at the calendar.

'I think my colleague will allow me to say that you will shortly see an improvement in his Lordship's condition.'

'Thank God for that,' they cried together.

'Now, if you please, Dr Grimsdyke, we shall return to your surgery.' He pulled out that great gold watch of his. 'We have really little time for discussion before the four o'clock train.'

Sir Lancelot didn't mention the patient on our way back to the uncle's cottage, being more interested in describing all the different methods of thatching. I had to wait till he was enjoying a cup of tea in the parlour, when he declared:

'Apart from an uncomplicated healing fracture, there's nothing whatever wrong with Lord Nutbeam. But there's one thing he needs desperately – an interest in life. Believe me, it's perfectly easy to be bored to death. What do you suggest?'

'More books, sir?'

Sir Lancelot seemed to find this amusing.

'From you, Grimsdyke, a remarkable answer. The advice about never judging others by yourself is one of the stupider of proverbs. If humanity didn't show an astounding sameness, the practice of medicine would come to a dead stop.'

He spread a scone with clotted cream and strawberry jam.

'I agree that after a lifetime playing the recluse, Lord Nutbeam's expedition to hospital was something of a shock. With the appalling advance of specialization, hospitals have become quite overcrowded with staff – it is, of course, completely impossible to get any rest in them. Did you notice his nurses?'

'As a matter of fact I did, sir. There was a staff nurse and – '

Sir Lancelot raised his hand. 'It is quite enough answer, Grimsdyke, that you noticed them. No doubt Lord Nutbeam finds the amateur ministrations of his sister-in-law less agreeable. I shall send down a qualified nurse from a London bureau tomorrow. You will see to it that she isn't overruled by the family.'

'That might be a bit difficult, sir.'

'Rubbish!' He helped himself to a slice of fruit cake. 'There's only one way to handle difficult patients, difficult relatives, and difficult horses, and that's by keeping on top. I hope my visit has clothed you with a little added authority. That's often the only value of the consultant appearing on the scene at all.'

'How about tonics, sir?'

'To my mind there is only one effective tonic. I shall arrange for that to be sent from London also. I think I have time for another cup of tea, if you please. By the by,' he went on, as I put down the pot. 'You knew your cousin Miles was putting up for the consultant staff at St Swithin's?'

'He did mention it to me, sir.'

'How's he fancy his chances?'

'I think he's modest by nature, sir,' I replied cagily.

'H'm. I am only betraying an open secret by saying that Cambridge is being remarkably difficult in the selection committee. Obstinacy is such an extremely unpleasing characteristic.' Sir Lancelot stroked his beard. 'How are your relations with your cousin?'

'We do rather move in different worlds, sir.'

'I don't know if you are sufficiently familiar to drop a hint that his chances at St Swithin's would be considerably bettered if he were a little more disgustingly human. Otherwise he's an exemplary candidate. His work has ability, his manner has confidence, and, what is more important, his wife has money. But whoever the committee elects, you have to live with the feller for the rest of your professional lifetime. And nothing is more trying than being yoked to a pillar of virtue, as you can find from the divorce courts any afternoon,'

'I'm sure Miles is dedicated to his profession, sir,' I remarked, taking the chance to slip in a good word for the chap.

'Nothing,' declared Sir Lancelot, 'is quite so dangerous as the dedicated man.' Shortly afterwards I drove him to the station. I no longer had any qualms about tackling the Nutbeams, even over the nurse.

'A nurse? That will be rather tedious, Doctor,' Amanda objected at once, 'We had one in the house before, the time my husband had pneumonia. It really was most difficult. They feel quite entitled to have their meals at the same table, and even attempt to sit with one in the evenings.'

This annoyed me more, because I'm a great admirer of the nursing profession, or at least of some of it. Remembering Sir Lancelot's advice, I said pretty stuffily, 'If you don't obey your doctor's orders, there really isn't much point in having one.'

'I assure you I can put up with any inconvenience for the sake of my brother-in-law's health,' she returned. 'I will instruct the housekeeper to prepare a room immediately.'

I myself wasn't much looking forward to sharing the clinical management of Lord Nutbeam with a nurse, knowing how Sir Lancelot's taste in them lay. His ward sisters at St Swithin's were a couple of women who could have kept Atila the Hun in bed for a month on bread-and-milk, and I expected someone about six feet tall with a chin like a football boot, old enough to have spanked Lord Nutbeam as a baby and tough enough to try it now. It was therefore with some astonishment that I arrived at Nutbeam Hall the next evening to discover the most beautiful girl I'd seen in my life.

'Good evening, Doctor,' she greeted me. 'I am Nurse Jones. I have given the patient his bath, and he is ready for you to see him now.'

I couldn't do anything except stare and bless my luck. She was a dainty, demure creature, with a little bow thing under her chin. She looked like Snow-White, just growing out of her dwarfs. I was hopeful that our professional relationship would quickly ripen into something more promising, the sub-postmistress being all very well for country rambles but having the annoying habit of continually explaining how you counted postal orders.

'Oh, jolly good,' I said. 'I hope you like it here in the country? Perhaps you'd care to see the local beauty spots one afternoon when you're off duty?'

She gave a smile as gentle as the ripples on the village pond.

'That is really most kind of you, Doctor, but I'm afraid I shan't find much time to spare with such an important case.'

'We'll see, eh?' Nothing brings a man and woman together like treating someone else's illnesses. 'Let's go and inspect his Lordship.'

I found Lord Nutbeam sitting in bed sipping a glass of champagne.

'Where on earth did that come from?' I exclaimed.

'But the note from Fortnum and Mason's said you'd ordered it for me, Doctor.'

'Oh, did I? Yes, of course I did. Bollinger, eh? Sir Lancelot's favourite tipple. Jolly good tonic, don't you find?'

'I would never take alcohol except on doctor's orders, of course. But I must say, it does make me feel extremely well. How much do you want me to drink of it, Doctor? I believe six dozen bottles arrived downstairs.'

I murmured something about a bottle a day keeping the doctor away, and invited myself to a drop.

'How do you like your new nurse?' I asked, as she disappeared to find a glass.

Lord Nutbeam thought for some moments.

'She reminds me of a little Crabbe.'

'She doesn't walk sideways,' I said, feeling this rather un-complimentary.

'"Courteous though coy, and gentle though retired," ' he quoted. ' "The joy of youth and health her eyes display'd. And ease of heart her every look convey'd." '

I felt that the case had taken a turn for the better.

11

Nurse Jones was a great success all round. In a couple of days she had old Nutbeam out of his wheel-chair tottering round sniffing the flowers. The next week she'd taken to driving him about the countryside of an afternoon in the Daimler. And, calling one lunch-time, I was surprised to see he'd gone off his usual diet of poached egg on pulverized spinach and was tucking into a steak the size of a bath-mat.

Even the Percy Nutbeams didn't object to the new régime, partly because his Lordship was every day in every way getting better and better, and partly because of the way Nurse Jones handled the missus. Nurses are charming girls, though unfortunately inclined to be bossy, doubtless the effect of spending their formative years telling old men to get back into bed. But Nurse Jones was as sweet and gentle as Gee's Linctus, and always took care to address Mrs Nutbeam like an Edwardian housemaid straight out of the orphanage.

'The nurse at least knows her place,' Amanda admitted to me one afternoon. 'Which is a very welcome discovery in anyone these days. Though, of course, she could hardly expect to mix with people of our class. Not only was she trained at some extremely obscure hospital, but her father, I believe, is an engine driver.'

'You mean in *loco parentis?*' I suggested. But Amanda Nutbeam definitely had no sense of humour, either.

"All the same, I'm glad Sir Lancelot Spratt recommended her. She seems to be doing his Lordship the world of good.'

She was doing me the world of good, too. After passing the day sticking penicillin into rural posteriors, you can't imagine how you look forward to half an hour with a civilized popsie in the evening.

'Good evening, Nurse Jones,' I would greet her at the bedroom door.

'And how is his Lordship this evening?'

'Very well, thank you, Doctor. He has taken his vitaminized milk and played *Clair de Lune* twice on the piano.'

'And how are *you*, Nurse Jones?'

'Very well, thank you, Doctor.'

'Perhaps one afternoon you would like a spot of fresh air and a view of the beauty spots, Nurse Jones?'

'Perhaps one afternoon, Doctor.'

After a week or two, I felt the time had come to put our acquaintance on a rather jollier footing.

Old Nutbeam had hobbled out of the room somewhere, and Nurse Jones had been listening very respectfully while I held forth on the osteopathology of uniting fractures, so I put my arm round her waist and kissed her.

The result was rather unexpected. I'd imagined that she'd drop her eyes and dissolve into grateful sobs on my waistcoat. Instead, she caught me a neat uppercut on the left ramus of the mandible.

I don't know if many people have been clocked by nurses, but quite a lot of power they pack, after all those years shifting patients about with their bare hands. She hit me clean off my balance, right into the remains of his Lordship's dinner. But I was even more startled at the appearance of little Nurse Jones herself. She looked as though she'd been charged with a powerful current of electricity. She was all eyes and teeth and fingernails.

'You despicable young man!' she hissed. 'Do you take me for one of your hospital pick-ups? Keep your hands to yourself, and your manners to the saloon bar,'

'I say, I'm most terribly sorry.' I brushed off the remains of a fruit salad. 'It was all meant in a perfectly friendly spirit. Like at Christmas.'

'Oh, I know you young doctors!' She looked as though she wanted to spit out something nasty. 'Do you imagine I put up with five years' hard labour in a hospital like a workhouse just for people like you to maul me about? Huh! I want more out of life than that. It's bad enough drudging away night and day, without having to defend yourself against ham-fisted Romeos as soon as you're left alone in the same room. You make me absolutely nauseated.'

Strong words, of course. But the Grimsdykes, I trust, are ever gentlemen, and sensitive to the first hint that their attentions might be unwelcome.

'A thousand apologies,' I told her, rather stiffly. 'It's all this hot weather we're having. I can assure you, Nurse Jones, that the incident will not occur again.'

'I can assure you, too,' she said.

At that moment old Nutbeam pottered back, and she became her usual demure self once more.

For the next few days I didn't know whether I was more confused than disappointed. After all, every houseman's tried a bit of slap-and-tickle in the sluice-room, and the worst response is usually a few remarks about not being that sort of a girl and Sister might come back in a minute, anyway. But Nurse Jones could look as if butter wouldn't melt in her mouth while comfortably able to digest red-hot nails. It was puzzling, and rather a shame. I'd been particularly looking forward to those beauty spots.

Arriving at Nutbeam Hall a few evenings later, I thought at first that Nurse Jones was in form again. Then I recognized the voices behind the drawing-room door.

'For a man in your position behaving like that with one of the servants,' Mrs Nutbeam was declaring, 'is absolutely disgusting.'

'My dear!' bleated Percy. 'She's hardly a servant – '

'Of course she's a servant. I've had lady's maids in the past who were twice as good as she is.'

'But my dear – '

'And in our own home, with your own brother lying ill in the next room. Really, Percy!'

'My dear – '

'You've always treated me atrociously, but this is too much. Far too much. Haven't I enough on my mind at this moment?'

'But, my dear, how was I to know she'd make such a fuss? I was only trying to hold her hand.'

'And you have the effrontery to offer that as an excuse! If I had my way I'd bundle the little baggage out of the house in the next five minutes. It's only that she's kept your brother out of his grave that I tolerate her at all.'

'Let me tell you, my dear, the scene won't be repeated.'

'And let me tell you, my dear, that if it is, I'll break your neck.'

It was quite a consolation to find that Nurse Jones dished it out impartially to all comers.

Thereafter I paid fewer visits to Nutbeam Hall, his Lordship no longer needing my constant attentions, anyway. There wasn't even much excitement for the Percy Nutbeams watching LSD-day approaching, as he quietly became haler and heartier every moment. Under the mellowing influence of the coming largesse the ghastly couple grew quite friendly towards me, and even asked me to a cocktail party with a lot of their friends, who looked as though they'd been delivered in horse-boxes,

At last the twenty-eighth of May dawned, another jolly Elysian summer day. In the afternoon I drove to Nutbeam Hall for my final visit.

I found Percy and his wife standing in the hall, looking as if they'd just checked off the winning line in their penny points.

'Dr Grimsdyke,' Percy said at once, 'we both want to thank you for restoring my dear brother to us.'

'It is a great comfort, Doctor, to have him with us today. And, of course, for many more years to come.'

'If God spares him,' added Percy, looking at the chandelier again.

'To mark our appreciation,' Amanda went on, 'my husband and I would like you to accept this little gift. I hope it will remind you of one of your earliest successful cases.'

Whereupon Percy handed me a gold cigarette case, still in its box from Cartiers.

I stumbled out a few words of thanks, wondering how much it had set them back. Then I suggested I'd better make my *adieus* to the patient himself.

'My brother's out for his afternoon drive at the moment,' Percy told me, 'but of course he's due home any minute.'

'He never likes to be far from Nutbeam Hall,' said Amanda.

'Do wait, Doctor. Perhaps a cup of tea?'

At that moment we heard the Daimler in the drive, and as we opened the front door Lord Nutbeam got out with Nurse Jones. It was then I noticed something about him – possibly the look in his eye, like a chap reaching for his first pint at the end of a tough game of rugger – which made me slip the cigarette case into my pocket and prepare for trouble.

'Percy…Amanda,' began Lord Nutbeam, 'allow me to introduce Lady Nutbeam.'

The two Honourables looked as though they'd been run through the middle by a red-hot cautery.

'That's impossible!' cried Mrs Nutbeam.

'Not impossible at all, my dear Amanda. Ethel and I were married half an hour ago in Gloucester Registry Office. Two very pleasant young men from the Waterworks Department were our witnesses.'

Percy Nutbeam gasped. 'But the money!'

'I'm afraid there isn't any, Percy. Not for you, anyway. The deed is, of course, annulled by my marrying before the five years are up. You will inherit the title when I eventually perish, unless Ethel and I happen to have children…'

Mrs Nutbeam burst into tears.

'But I doubt whether there will be much money left, because I intend to spend it. I realize now how I have wasted my life, because you two cleverly insisted on keeping me under your noses. I'm not at all delicate. Ethel tells me I'm as vigorous as any man of twenty. I knew I'd been missing something, ever since I was among all those nice young people in hospital.'

Lord Nutbeam smiled benignly all round.

'Dear Doctor, do you recall I once mentioned Gray's *Elegy in a Country Churchyard*? I was about to quote – "Full many a flower is born to blush unseen, And waste its sweetness on the desert air." Charming poem. Well, I'm going to blush all over the place from now on. Ethel and I are off tomorrow for our honeymoon at Monte Carlo. You must come, Doctor, and visit me then when we've settled down. You probably prefer to stay here, Percy. And so you may, if you wish. Until we get back.'

'Don't forget the present, darling,' said Lady Nutbeam, looking as unruffled as when she changed his Lordship's pyjamas.

'Ah, the present. It was you, Doctor, who brought dear Ethel and I together. So perhaps you will accept this little token of our lasting gratitude and affection?'

And he handed me a gold cigarette case, still in its box from Cartiers,

12

'I don't believe a word of it,' said Miles.

'Don't you indeed?' I replied, and produced a couple of identical gold cigarette cases from my pockets.

'The only snag is knowing what to do with the things, my life never being organized to meet such a situation. I think I'll reserve one for the hock shop, and have the other engraved "With Gratitude From a Successful Patient." Then I can offer people cigarettes from it, and do my professional standing no end of good. Though I suppose I might as well have "With Gratitude from Her Royal Highness" while I'm about it, don't you think?'

I'd left Long Wotton that morning to the touching distress of everybody, particularly the sub-postmistress, who burst into tears and gummed up all the threepenny stamps. Even the old uncle had congratulated me on handling the Nutbeams, and not only written a comfortable cheque as promised but given me a straw hat from Jamaica. Percy Nutbeam himself had smartly disappeared from the district, it was rumoured to sell cars in a Piccadilly showroom, and I'd half a mind to go along later and make faces through the plate-glass window.

It was a beautiful afternoon in the middle of Ascot week as I arrived in London, when even the chaps with placards announcing Doom is Nigh at the bottom of the Edgware Road looked as though the world wasn't such a bad old place after all. I was sorry to find the only drab patch on the whole cheerful canvas of life was poor old Miles himself.

'They've postponed the appointment at St Swithin's for six months,' he announced, not seeming really interested in cigarette cases. 'The committee have invited Professor Kaiser from Kentucky to fill the gap with a clinical visit.'

'Gloved hands across the sea, and all that?'

He snorted. 'Not a bit of it! It's nothing but a transparent ruse for everyone to organize their forces. My only encouragement is that Mr Longfellow from the Neurosurgical Department is now supporting me. Though, of course, he always opposes Sir Lancelot in everything.'

'Because Sir Lancelot gave him out, umpiring the last Staff and Students cricket match.'

'I shouldn't be at all surprised at that.' Miles stared gloomily at the print of Luke Fildes' *The Doctor*. 'If only the patients knew what went on behind their backs!'

'Why don't you and Connie get away from it all and take a holiday?' I suggested. 'The yearly change of scene is essential for mental and bodily health – lesson one, social medicine.'

'Nothing depresses me quite so much as packing.'

'But the sunny shores of the Mediterranean – '

'Only seem to give me the gut-rot.'

I'd thought of passing on Sir Lancelot's advice. but the poor fellow looked so hopelessly miserable I said instead, 'Don't worry about me, old lad. I'll do my bit by staying out of sight and out of trouble. At least for the next six months.'

'You know, Gaston, you're... you're being rather decent about all this.'

'Not at all. One of the family, good cause, and all that.'

'I'm sincerely grateful to you. If can be any help in finding a new position – '

'Not necessary, old lad. I have a scheme which will take me right out of everybody's hair for a bit.'

'You're not emigrating?' I thought his voice sounded a little too hopeful. 'Apart from the oil company, I know the Secretary of the Commonwealth Resettlement Board pretty well at the club. He could easily fix you up somewhere like Australia or Canada.'

I shook my head. 'Worthy places all, but I shall remain based on this blessed plot. What was it old Sir Lancelot used to tell us? "I know one-half of this country thinks it's underpaid and the other half that it's over-taxed, but believe me, gentlemen, it's cheap at the price." Anyway, my immediate future is taken care of in the homeland.'

'Respectably, I trust?'

'Very. But I must maintain strict professional secrecy about it at the moment.'

Miles looked surprised, but asked no more questions. We parted on such excellent terms I wished afterwards I'd thought of asking him for another ten quid.

I didn't enlighten Miles that I was planning to write a book, because he would have told me it was a stupid notion, and I should have agreed with him. Though a good many other doctors seem to have had the same idea – Oliver Goldsmith, Smollett, Rabelais, Conan Doyle, Somerset Maugham, and so on. The thought had come to me in the uncle's study at Long Wotton, where I'd been browsing to keep up with Lord Nutbeam's conversation. Half-way through *The World's Ten Great Novels* it struck me that a chap who could write the obituaries for the *Medical Observer* ought to be pretty good at producing convincing fiction.

The only snag was paying the rent while writing it, and I suppose the same problem worried Goldsmith and Smollett as well. But now I had the uncle's cheque I could afford to take a small houseboat in Chelsea, if I managed to live largely on baked beans and benzedrine.

The next afternoon I'd an appointment with some publishers called Carboy and Plover in Bloomsbury, a district with high-class literary associations but now consisting of small hotels for drunk Scotsmen missing the night trains from King's Cross.

'A hospital story, eh? They're generally sellers, at any rate,' said Mr Carboy.

He was a fat chap in a tweed suit, whom I'd found sitting among photographs of his best-selling authors and prize-winning cattle reading the *Farmer and Stockbreeder*. But he was very civil, and gave me a cup of tea.

'The drama of the operating theatre,' murmured Plover, a thin, pale fellow on whom nothing seemed to grow very well – hair, moustache, bow-tie, all drooped like a sensitive plant after a thunderstorm,

'I'll have a go, then,' I said. I felt the interview was more encouraging than the one you got on entering St Swithin's, when they just told you the number of chaps they chucked out for slacking.

'Have a go by all means, Doctor,' agreed Carboy. 'Just send us the manuscript when it's finished. Can't promise anything definite, of course. But we'll certainly read it.'

'Er – one small point – '

I didn't want to raise sordid questions among such literary gents, but I went on, 'I met an author chap once, who said publishers often made a small advance – '

'We should be delighted, Doctor,' said Carboy. 'Absolutely delighted,' agreed Plover. 'Nothing gives a publisher greater pleasure than encouraging the young artist. Eh, Plover? But alas! The state of the book trade,'

'Simply terrible just now,' affirmed Plover, drooping further.

'Quite indescribable.'

'Bankruptcies weekly.'

'Poor Hargreaves. Shot himself only yesterday.'

'I'm not at all certain,' ended Plover, 'that I didn't hear the crack of a pistol shot on my way to lunch.'

I left, wondering whether I should offer to pay for the tea.

In the absence of patronage from Carboy and Plover, I put one cigarette case up the spout, bought a second-hand typewriter and Roget's *Thesaurus*, and settled down to work.

Being a medical student is jolly good training for becoming an author. In both occupations you have to sit at a desk for hours on end when you'd rather be out in the pubs, and to live on practically nothing. Though I must admit it was only late in the course that I developed this knack for the studious life. The old uncle had become even stickier with the money after a surprise visit to my new digs one evening, when the landlady answered his question, 'Is this where Mr Grimsdyke lives?' with, 'That's right, sir, bring 'im in and mind 'is poor 'ead on the doorstep.'

I also found that writing a book, like taking out an appendix, looks rather easier from the appearance of the finished product than it is. The snag in writing a book about hospitals is that everyone imagines the atmosphere inside resembles the closing stages of a six-day bicycle race, while the operating theatre is really a relaxed and friendly place, like a well-run garage. Also, the public thinks all surgeons are high-principled and handsome, though most of them are little fat men with old pyjamas under their operating gowns, mainly worried about getting the next hernia done in time to have a decent lunch. My hero, one Clifford Standforth, *FRCS*, was a brilliant, upright, serious young surgeon, and somehow he didn't seem the sort of chap who'd last half an hour at St Swithin's without getting his leg pulled by everyone down to the first-year students.

After a few weeks, with foolscap on the floor as thick as the snow on a Christmas card, I found myself like any other hermit in pressing need of a decent meal and some conversation, and I invited myself round to Miles' flat for dinner. I thought I could finally pass on Sir Lancelot's remarks about slapping chaps on the back a bit more, but I found the fellow in an even deeper condition of acute melancholia.

'What's up now?' I asked. 'Sir Lancelot still creating about that car park?'

'Barefoot,' Miles replied.

'Oh,' I said.

'He's putting up for the job, too.'

'Unfortunate,' I agreed.

'Everything's against me,' muttered Miles. 'I thought the fellow had settled down for life as Reader in Surgery at West Riding.'

'He's your only serious rival, I suppose?'

'As ever,' agreed Miles bitterly. 'You've never said a word, I suppose. Gaston? Not about the true story?'

I shook my head. 'Not evens to Connie.'

'Thank you, Gaston. I appreciate that deeply.'

I felt so unhappy for him I had to help myself to some of his whisky and soda. The Barefoot incident was the only shady part of old Miles' rather sad salad days. Everyone at St Swithin's thought it pretty mysterious at the time, the general rumour being that the poor chap had suffered a nervous breakdown following years of chronic overwork, which was highly gratifying to students like myself who believed in long periods of recuperation between exams.

It all happened just before Miles went up for his finals before either of us had yet run into Connie. Charlie Barefoot was a small, untidy pink chap who resembled a cherub in glasses, and the pair of them had met their first week in St Swithin's, over that beastly dogfish.

'I say, isn't that Hume's *Treatise on Human Nature* you have there?' asked Miles, waiting for the class to start one morning.

Barefoot nodded. 'I like to keep my mind occupied while I'm hanging about for anything – trains, haircuts, scholarship exams, and so on. But isn't that Darwin's *Origin of Species?'*

Miles said it was. 'I thought it a useful start to one's medical education.'

'But I've been waiting for months to discuss Darwin's views on natural selection!'

'And I've been waiting for months to discuss Hume's views on subjective idealism!'

After that they were great pals.

Medical students in the first year have hardly shaken the schoolroom chalk from their shoulders, but they soon learn to crowd the rear benches of the lecture-room so that unobtrusive exits might be made should the subject start to pall. Miles and Barefoot were always left with the front row to themselves, where they answered all the questions, took notes by the armful, and generally gave the impression intellectually of a pair of young Mozarts. At the end of the first year Miles won the Dean's Prize in Biology, with Charlie Barefoot *proxime accessit*.

That got rid of the dogfish, by promotion from the medical kindergarden to the anatomy rooms. They shared the same leg.

'Miles, I've got some capital news,' Barefoot announced, as my cousin arrived one morning. 'There's a vacancy in my digs. Tony Benskin doesn't want to stay any longer. I don't know why, but he got quite shirty the other day, just because I wanted to discuss the popliteal fossa over breakfast. If you were thinking of making a change – '

'I'll give my landlady notice tonight,' Miles replied at once. 'My lodgings are really very difficult for studying in the evenings. Quite apart from the noise of Paddington Station, there are a couple of ladies on my landing who seem to have a tremendous succession of visitors.'

'You'll find it much more agreeable at Muswell Hill. Mrs Capper provides use of the parlour and lets us make cocoa as late as we like in the evening.'

Miles moved his books and bones across London, and from Monday to Friday every night afterwards the pair of them swotted at Mrs Capper's parlour table. On Saturdays they went for a long walk in the country and took supper at Lyons'. In time, Miles won the Gold Medal in Anatomy, with Barefoot again runner-up.

By the time I'd shaken off the blasted dogfish myself, Miles and Barefoot were already at work in the St Swithin's wards. Despite the standing impression of hospital inmates, medical students are let loose on live patients only after a couple of years of cutting up dead ones, and a pretty testing transition it is, too. A good many bright young anatomists I've seen floundering about among the dirty dressings and vomit bowls, and they say all the best surgeons were as hopeless at anatomy as all the best judges were at law. But even Sir Lancelot Spratt agreed it was simply a matter of time before Miles won the University Prize in Surgery, with Barefoot as usual panting a few marks behind.

Then a most unusual dislocation nobbled this pair of academic steeplechasers.

When I started in the hospital myself, I found that once you'd sorted out the odd sounds that come rumbling up a stethoscope the greatest difficulty in a medical ward is not making a diagnosis but making a bed. Hospital sisters regard the students as farmers regard their own unavoidable pests, and insist on all blankets being replaced complete with official hospital corners, which was totally beyond old Miles. He couldn't examine a patient without leaving him like a finisher in a sack-race.

After inspecting a particularly tricky case of splenomegaly one evening, Miles was struggling to tuck back the foot of the bed without repeatedly folding his tie into it, when a voice behind him said softly, 'If you let me do it, perhaps it would be easiest for both of us in the end?'

My cousin found a small, blonde junior nurse smiling at him.

'Awfully decent of you,' he stammered.

'You're working terribly late, aren't you?'

She gave the bed-cover a professional flick.

'Oh, I don't know. I rather like work. You new on the ward?'

'I came down from ENT yesterday. My name's Nurse Crimpole.'

'Mine's Miles Grimsdyke.'

'Of course I knew that.'

'You did?'

'Surely everyone in the hospital has heard of the clever Miles Grimsdyke. Quite unlike the other one.'

She gave him another smile. Miles' stomach felt as though he'd swallowed a nest of glow-worms.

'What would you enumerate as the differential diagnosis of acute nephritis?' asked Charlie Barefoot across Mrs Capper's red-plush tablecloth later that evening.

Miles switched his eyes from Mr Capper's Buffalo Group over the fireplace.

'Eh?'

'You all right?' Barefoot looked concerned. 'You haven't touched your cocoa.'

'Yes, I'm fine, thanks. Fit as a flea. Though perhaps I'm overdoing the Saturday tramps a little. Sorry, old man.'

'It wasn't important. Anything interesting happen in the ward this evening?'

'No. Nothing worth mentioning at all,' said Miles.

13

The next Saturday Miles told Barefoot he was visiting his aunt in Sydenham, and took Nurse Crimpole to the pictures.

'You really mustn't work so hard,' she murmured, as he held her hand afterwards outside the mortuary gate. 'I shouldn't like anything to happen to you.'

'Perhaps I'll cut down in the evenings a bit, Dulcie. The finals aren't for a couple of years yet, anyway.'

'And I'm sure you're not getting nearly enough to eat.'

'Mrs Capper's a bit mean with the first-class proteins, I must say.'

'Do look after yourself. Miles – won't you?' She looked into his eyes and stroked his lapel. 'For my sake.'

Next week Miles told Barefoot he was visiting his uncle in Beckenham, and took Nurse Crimpole to the Palladium.

For once in his life old Miles found he couldn't concentrate. Unlike myself, whose thoughts tend to wander from the books in the direction of Lord's or Epsom, Miles could not control his brain like a prize fighter his muscles. But now Nurse Crimpole's smile kept coming between him and such things as the electrocardiographic diagnosis of Fallot's tetrology. No nurse had wasted her time on the poor chap before, with such grand people as housemen and registrars about in the ward, Come to think of it, no woman had wasted her time on him at all. I wish I'd known what was going on. I might have buttonholed the chap and offered some fatherly advice.

Miles decided the next Saturday to tell Barefoot he was visiting his nephew in Croydon, and take Nurse Crimpole to the Corner House.

When he slipped into the ward sluice-room to issue the invitation, he was surprised to discover her chatting to his room-mate.

'Just looking for my diabetic specimens,' Miles said quickly.

'They've been taken down to the path. lab., old man,' Charlie Barefoot told him. 'If you're going that way, I'll come along and collect my own. Bye-bye, Dulcie,' he added to Nurse Crimpole. 'See you on Saturday.'

'Two o'clock outside the Nurses' Home,' she replied, and went on polishing her bedpans.

Miles felt he'd been given the electroconvulsive treatment he'd seen in the psychiatric department. It had never occurred to the idiot that Dulcie Crimpole could have eyes for anyone else – particularly, he felt angrily, a stodgy old bookworm like Charlie Barefoot.

'Known Nurse Crimpole long?' he asked in the pathology laboratory, his hand trembling as he unstoppered a bottle of Benedict's reagent.

'I've seen her about the ward, you know.'

Miles paused.

'I didn't go to my relatives those last week-ends,' he scowled.

'So she tells me.'

'I think Dulcie's a very nice girl.'

'So do I,' said Charlie Barefoot.

That evening, Miles glanced up sharply from his Muir's *Pathology* and said, 'Perhaps, Barefoot, you would have the kindness to return my pencil, when you've finished chewing it.'

'This happens to be my own pencil, Grimsdyke. And I am *not* chewing it.'

'I distinctly saw you chew it just now. Apart from ruining the pencil – my pencil – you ought to know that chewing pencils is a thoroughly unhygienic habit, leading to the transfer of *Streptococcus viridans* and large numbers of other oral pathogens.'

'Oh, take the bloody pencil!' said Barefoot, and went up and sat in his bedroom.

It was the old business of sex. Cut-throat rivalry in class had never ruffled the two chaps' friendship. Now they glared at each other all night across the top of their textbooks. The following Saturday evening, Miles sat alone miserably drinking cups of cocoa and wondering blackly how to do Charlie Barefoot down. The Saturday afterwards he told his chum he was taking Dulcie to the Festival Hall, and visited her parents in Guildford. On the Monday morning the whole hospital discovered that he and Nurse Crimpole were engaged.

Barefoot was very decent about it.

'I won't say I am not disappointed,' he confessed in Mrs Capper's parlour. 'Dulcie's a wonderful girl, and I was getting rather fond of her. But…well, there's no one I'd rather lose her to than you, Miles,'

'It's really extremely generous of you, Charlie.'

'And when's the wedding?'

'Not till I've qualified, of course, I've cabled my father out East that my new status certainly won't interfere with my work. You'll be my best man, I hope?'

'That will be my only consolation for the whole affair.'

'You're a brick, Charlie.'

'And you're a real sport, Miles,'

They shook hands across Eden & Holland's *Obstetrics*.

'Now,' began Charlie Barefoot. 'What would you consider the leading features in the management of a case of puerperal paranoia?'

The years which stretch pretty chillingly ahead of you as a junior medical student soon start to melt away. As far as I remember, after that Miles took Dulcie out regularly every Saturday, while Barefoot went by himself for tramps in the country. The rest of the week the pair of them studied as steadily as before.

'You'll collar the Medical and Surgical Prizes in the finals all right,' conceded Barefoot, when the exams were only a few weeks ahead.

Miles smiled across the plush tablecloth, now a little faded.

'It could easily be your turn, Charlie.'

Barefoot shook his head. 'No, Miles. You're streets ahead of me on the practical. But I suppose we'd both better get on with some work. There's really so much revision to get through. What are the ninety-four causes of haematuria?'

When Miles next met Dulcie, he explained he couldn't spare his Saturday afternoons from studying any longer.

'But you really must get some fresh air,' she insisted. 'After all, now I'm a staff nurse and know all about these things. Lack of sunlight can reduce your vitamin D right down to danger-level.'

'Damn vitamin D!' exclaimed Miles. 'And A, B, and C as well.'

'Miles!' she said, horrified at such blasphemy.

'I'm sorry, dear. I'm a bit irritable these days. It's only the pressure of work.'

'Are you sure that's all? You're looking terribly peaky.'

'Yes, of course that's all.'

Old Miles is fundamentally honest, which has nearly wrecked more careers than his own. He disliked telling Dulcie a lie. But how could he explain that he wished the ruddy woman were dead? A couple of years in the rough-and-tumble of the hospital wards has changed far worldlier young fellows than my cousin. As a junior student he'd been surprised at any girl smiling at him. Now he was almost a doctor and got smiles all round, some of them very pretty ones. And he could no longer dissuade himself that the woman was a shocking bore.

'Are you sure you're getting enough sleep?' Dulcie went on. 'The Professor says seven hours is the normal minimum. And what about your diet? I'm certain you're not taking nearly enough calories. Dr Parsons gave us a smashing lecture about them yesterday.'

'Very interesting, dear. How would you like to pass the afternoon? Shall we go round an art gallery?'

'If you don't think it would tire you too much. From the way you walk about, Miles, I'm not at all sure you haven't got flat feet.'

The wedding was planned for a fortnight after the examinations, and I was already wondering how to raise the rent of a Moss Bros. suit. I hadn't seen anything of Miles for weeks, and supposed he was swotting steadily for the exam. In fact, he was mostly sitting in Mrs Capper's parlour trying to find some honourable escape from his obligations short of suicide. After my own later experiences in Porterhampton, I could sympathize with the chap. He told me afterwards he'd almost reached for Murrell's *Poisons* before the answer appeared, with the clarity of all great inspirations.

Miles decided deliberately to fail his exam.

Even I could appreciate the simplicity of the scheme. Miles couldn't sit again for another six months, and by then Dulcie Crimpole might have got tired of waiting. She might have got a sister's job miles away in the North. She might have got run over by an ambulance. At least he wouldn't be walking up the aisle with her in exactly six weeks' time.

'Hello!' exclaimed Barefoot, arriving home from his tramp in the Chilterns. 'You're looking much happier with life tonight.'

Personally, I always find the day of the examinations as unattractive as the Day of Judgement, but Miles and Barefoot strode into the examination hall a few weeks later without flinching.

'Good luck, Miles,' whispered Barefoot, as they separated among the schoolroom desks just far enough apart to make cribbing rather tantalizing.

My cousin smiled, 'This time you don't need any, Charlie.'

Miles told me he did well in the written paper – bottling up that knowledge from Mrs Capper's parlour would have been almost as heartbreaking for him as marrying Nurse Crimpole. Besides, the clinical session presents more opportunities for spectacular failure under the eye of the examiner himself. When a few mornings later Miles approached the bedside of his allotted examination case, he felt both determined and serene.

'Well, my boy,' began the examiner, appearing after the interval they give you for diagnosis, 'what do you find wrong with your patient?'

'I am afraid, sir,' said Miles, 'that I can't make a diagnosis of anything at all.'

The examiner seized him by the hand.

'Congratulations! We've put in a perfectly normal man, and you'd be horrified at the peculiar diagnoses I've had to put up with all morning. Mr Miles Grimsdyke, isn't it? I thought so. Only a student of your outstanding ability could have seen through our little deception. Excellent, my dear sir! Good morning.'

Poor old Miles staggered into the street, gripped by an alarming thought – after all those years of being an academic athlete it was impossible for him to fail an examination at all. He made his way from the hall in a daze, wondering what the devil to do. There was still the oral examination that afternoon. He'd half a mind simply to clear off to the cinema instead, but they'd only give him another appointment like a candidate taken ill. The vision of Nurse Crimpole rose before him, wearing a wedding dress.

When he finally focused on his surroundings, he found himself facing a sign announcing THE RED LION – Ales and Spirits.

I don't believe Miles had ever swallowed a drink in his life, but he felt so miserable he decided to experiment with the treatment he'd seen me administering to myself for years.

'Good morning, sir,' said the chap behind the bar. 'What can I get you?'

'I want a drink.'

'Of course, sir. What sort of drink?'

It had never occurred to Miles that there were different ones.

He noticed an advertisement showing bottles glistening on blocks of ice, which looked very refreshing.

'A drink of that,'

'Vodka, sir? Large or small?'

'Oh. large, please. I didn't have time for my second cup of tea at breakfast.'

The story of Miles' oral examination never got out. No one likes a bit of gossip better than me, but even I should have felt a cad so much as hinting about it. His answers to Sir Lancelot Spratt at first flew across the green-baize table, even though he was grasping it for support as he wiped away the perspiration with his handkerchief.

'Now, Mr Grimsdyke,' went on Sir Lancelot, perfectly used to the oddities of nervous candidates, 'let us discuss the subject of gastric pain.'

'No,' said Miles.

'I beg your pardon?'

'I said no. You're always discussing gastric pain. And do you know why? I'll tell you. It's because you know all about gastric pain. You might know sweet Fanny Adams about anything else, as far as your students are concerned. You've bored me stiff with gastric pain for three years, and I'm not going to talk about it now.'

'You're perfectly correct, Mr Grimsdyke,' agreed Sir Lancelot after a thoughtful pause. 'Of all dead horses to flog, dead hobby horse are the worse. I'm glad that a gentleman of your courage had the decency to stop me becoming a tyrannical bore on the subject. Thank you. We shall discuss nausea and vomiting instead.'

'Oh, God!' said Miles, and gripped his waist coat.

He still might have passed if he hadn't been sick into Sir Lancelot's Homburg.

The next evening the pass-list was read from the examination hall steps, with the announcement that Charles Barefoot (St Swithin's) had won the University Prizes in Medicine and Surgery. Miles wasn't mentioned at all.

He'd arranged to meet Dulcie Crimpole outside Swan and Edgar's, and hurried to detonate his news. But before he could speak she held out her hand and said:

'Good-bye, Miles.'

'Good-bye?'

'Yes.' She felt for her handkerchief. 'I – I'm afraid I've been a bad girl. I'm very fond of you, Miles, but – I'm really in love with Charlie Barefoot after all. Now we want to get married.'

Miles gasped. 'But – but how long has this been going on?'

'Just a few weeks. I've been out with him every Saturday, while you studied at home. But I didn't want to tell you before. I thought it might upset you for your examination.'

14

'Even Sir Lancelot himself doesn't know the full story about Dulcie Crimpole,' Miles whispered on the doorstep, as I left for the houseboat after dinner. 'I believe I read in an advertisement somewhere that vodka leaves no smell on the breath...'

I nodded. 'A wise choice at the time.'

'Having such a formidable rival for the job as Barefoot is bad enough as it is. But if the tale got out just at this particular moment – '

'Rely on Gaston, old lad. Compared with me an oyster is garrulous. Besides, I have problems enough of my own.'

'Not serious, I hope?'

'Purely professional, and happily resolving every moment.'

He frowned slightly. 'What exactly *are* you up to, Gaston ?'

'One day I hope you'll find out. Meanwhile, don't worry. I'll take any odds you end up with a permanent stable at St Swithin's.'

'It's certainly kind of you to give me some encouragement. I'm afraid I don't seem to get much of it these days.'

Dinner had been pretty gloomy that evening, with Miles brooding on Barefoot and even Connie hardly able to raise a laugh when I told a few funny stories to cheer them up. Falling into the prevailing mood, I started pondering on my own troubles with the book. Then I suddenly had another of those brilliant inspirations of mine. Here I was, stuck over portraying to the public the brilliant and dedicated young surgeon. And sitting opposite glaring into his raspberries was the prototype, known intimately from childhood. Whenever my Clifford Standforth was faced with a tricky situation I had only to ask myself, 'How would that chump

Miles have tackled it?' and that should be good for another twenty pages. I was so taken with the idea I could hardly finish my coffee before hurrying back and trying it out on the typewriter.

I felt I could have the manuscript on Carboy and Plover's doormat in a fortnight, which I might have done if a telegram hadn't arrived a few days later from my forwarding address saying:

COME IMMEDIATELY MONTE CARLO ALL EXPENSES PAID.
LADY NUTBEAM.

The summons wasn't a particular surprise. I'd been following-up my former patient closely, this being easy from the newspaper placards, which generally said something like LORD NUTBEAM AGAIN. The old boy was whooping it up on the Riviera at a rate which made Champagne Charlie look very small beer, and people read so much about him on the bus going home he'd become one of the things the British public wondered how on earth they existed without, like penicillin and television.

I'm not one to refuse a free trip even to Margate, and anyway the houseboat had sprung a leak which I'd calculated in another ten days would put me completely under water. But I hesitated, wondering if Lord Nutbeam should have summoned a more high-powered doctor than myself. Finally, I decided that if he really wanted my own humble ministrations I couldn't let the old boy down, and stuffing my manuscript and stethoscope into a suitcase I rapidly switched professions and booked on the next plane south.

The following afternoon found me driving in his Lordship's new Rolls among the palm trees.

'It was Aubrey who insisted on sending for you,' said Lady Nutbeam, greeting me at her hotel. She looked just the same, except for the diamonds. 'He doesn't trust foreign doctors.'

'Are you sure he shouldn't have got the President of the Royal College of Physicians instead?'

'Not at all, Doctor. After all, you've saved his life once already, haven't you?'

I found old Nutbeam lying in a darkened room, suffering from nothing worse than a chronic hangover. Fortunately, I have wide clinical experience of this condition, and prescribed a diet of dry biscuits with some French spa water that tasted like bottled gasworks.

'That's a relief,' Lady Nutbeam agreed, as we left him suffering in peace. 'Though I didn't think it was anything serious. But I hope the poor dear will soon be himself again. He's so enjoying life at the moment.'

'He was rather out of training for it, that's all.'

'Perhaps you could stay on a few days, Doctor?' She paused on the terrace, gazing at the millionaires' yachts parked in the harbour as thickly as the cars on Brighton front. 'As a matter of fact, I *am* a little worried about my husband.'

'You mean,' I suggested, 'that party I read about in the papers? Pouring champagne over the Maharajah?'

She nodded. 'And setting off fireworks under the Greek millionaire. Not to mention the ice–cream down the French ballet dancer's dress. I'm afraid, Doctor, Aubrey might sometimes strike one as a little childish.'

'Pure boyish high spirits, I'm sure.'

'I should like to think so. I'd be much obliged if you'd keep an eye on him for a while. You might be able to control him a little. You know he thinks the world of your advice. You would be our guest, of course.'

I gathered the Nutbeams, and a good many other people in Monte Carlo, had cash in lands where you didn't have to fill in beastly little forms to get it out.

'I could possibly spare a day or two,' I admitted, 'if you're still sure I'm the right chap?'

'But you've learned the penalty of boyish high spirits already, Doctor, haven't you?' Lady Nutbeam smiled. 'I noticed in Long Wotton you took the lesson to heart.'

As the days went by and nobody asked me to leave, I found myself a regular member of Lord Nutbeam's household, along with the chauffeur and the valet. Come to think of it, I'd always wanted the job of private physician to a travelling millionaire, though these days there's as much chance of finding anybody travelling with their private executioner.

His Lordship being an easy patient, I passed the time sitting in the sun, finishing my book, and brushing up my French – I flatter myself I'm rather hot stuff at this *défense de crâcher* and *crêpes Suzette* business.

'*Garçon*,' I was saying fluently after a week or so, '*apportez-moi une verre du bon vieux biére anglaise, s'il vous plait*. And if that's the luncheon menu you have there, I'll try the *gratin de langoustines Georgette*. That's sort of mucked-up shrimps, isn't it?'

'*Monsieur* has the true English sense of humour.'

'Remind me sometime to tell you the story of *l'évêque et le perroquet*. Were the roses sent to the young lady I met in the Sporting Club last night?'

'*Mais certainement, monsieur*.'

'*Jolli bon spectacle*. And waiter – inform the chauffeur I'll be taking the car this afternoon. I might do a little shopping in Nice.'

'*Entendu, monsieur*.'

I felt that life for Grimsdyke was looking up.

The waiter had hardly left the terrace to collect my midmorning refreshment, when my patient himself appeared. Lord Nutbeam seemed in excellent spirits, and was smoking a cigar.

'My dear Doctor, when on earth are you going to let me have a drink?' he started as usual. 'I was passing such a delightful time going through the barman's cocktails. I'd just reached that most interesting concoction of tomato juice and vodka. There is so much to catch up on in life!'

'Next Monday you might run to a glass of *vin blanc*,' I told him sternly.

'But Doctor, the Film Festival ! It starts tomorrow, and I do so want to give a little party for those bright young people. I've never met a real film star, you know. Indeed, the only one I remember is a dog called Rin-tin-tin. I don't expect he'll be coming, of course.'

He offered me a cigar.

'They say *this* young lady is arriving at the hotel from London this afternoon,' he added, picking up a magazine with Melody Madder on the cover.

It was difficult at the time to pick up any magazine that hadn't. She was a red-head in a tight dress, Who – not to put too fine a point on it – struck me as suffering from pronounced mammary hyperplasia. But it seems a condition in which people are widely interested, and in the past few months she'd become better known to the British public than the Britannia on the back of a penny.

'Fascinating creature,' mused Lord Nutbeam. 'Remarkable how the point of interest changes, isn't it? Forty year's ago it was all legs, and forty years before that the girls wore bustles. I do so hope I shall live to see what it is next.

'The odd thing is,' I remarked, 'I've a feeling I've met her somewhere. I suppose I saw her in a picture.'

'I only wish you had met her, Doctor. I should so much like the pleasure of doing so myself, though Ethel seems most unenthusiastic at the idea. If you could ask her to my party I should certainly express my appreciation tangibly. You haven't a Rolls, have you?'

I promised to do my best.

'And how is the book coming along? Alas! For some reason I seem to be getting so behind with my reading these days.'

For the past couple of days the hotel had been steadily filling up for the Festival, mostly with actresses who were more or less overdressed or more or less undressed and all anatomically impossible, actors holding their breath while photographed in bathing-trunks, and film stars' husbands discussing their wives' income tax. The rest I supposed were the financial wizards, who could be spotted through their habit of approaching closed doors with their hands in their pockets, with about fifteen people fighting to grab the handle first.

It didn't seem easy to make the acquaintance of such a high-powered hotsie as Melody Madder, even if we were staying in the same hotel. I didn't even see more of her arrival than the top of her famous red hair, what with all the chaps trying to take her photograph. I found a quiet corner of the lobby and searched for a plan to present her with his Lordship's invitation. There wasn't much point in simply going along with a bunch of flowers, even Lord Nutbeam's name not cutting much ice with the woman who'd become as much a national institution as the lions in Trafalgar Square. I supposed I could send up an elegant little note, which at least might produce her autograph in return. As the first step seemed finding her room number, I was approaching the reception desk trying to remember the French for 'suite' when I was elbowed aside by a fat woman in a hat with cherries dangling from it.

'It's an utter disgrace,' the fat woman started on the unfortunate chap behind the counter. 'Our room's that stuffy I daren't draw a breath. Hasn't been aired for years, if you ask me. And as for the beds, I don't even like to think about them.'

'But if *madame* will open the shutters — '

'Open them? You try and open them. You'll have to use dynamite.'

I was a bit annoyed at the elbowing, though I saw her point — fresh air is provided free in English hotels, all round the windows and under the doors, but in France they get some inside a bedroom and like to keep it for years.

'And another thing. The light won't go on and I got stuck in the lift.'

'The hotel engineer will attend to it at once, *madame*.'

'As for the plumbing, it's disgraceful. What's the idea of that ridiculous wash-basin six inches off the ground ? Sir Theodore Theobald shall hear about this, believe you me. Furthermore, my daughter is still airsick, and I must have a doctor at once.'

'A doctor, Mrs Madder ? We shall send for the best available.'

I pushed myself forward.

'Forgive my butting in,' I said quickly, 'but if you want a doctor, I happen to be the chap.'

She looked as if I were another of the local inconveniences.

"The gentleman, *madame*, is personal physician to Lord Nutbeam.'

'Oh, are you? Well, I suppose you'll do. But I don't mind telling you here and now you can't expect any fancy fees.'

'In an emergency, Mrs Madder, it would be quite unethical for me to make a charge.'

This seemed to tip the scales, and I felt pretty pleased with myself as I followed her into the lift and up to a bedroom stuffed with flowers. Not only could I issue old Nutbeam's invitation as I felt Melody Madder's pulse, but I might be able to go over her chest as well.

'Get yourself ready, my girl,' said Mrs Madder, advancing to the bed. 'I've brought the doctor.'

'Good Lord!' I exclaimed. 'Why hello, Petunia.'

15

Petunia gave a little shriek and sat up in bed.

'Gaston! What on earth are you doing here?'

'But what are you doing here? In that hair, too.'

'What's all this?' demanded Mother.

'Mum, it's Dr Grimsdyke – you know, the one who used to bring me home in the rattly old car.'

'Oh, it is, is it? Yes, I remember now. I've often seen him from the bedroom window.'

'You seem to have come up a bit in the world, Pet,' I observed warmly. 'Jolly good job you didn't get the mumps after all.'

I kicked myself for not recognizing all those photographs. Though I must say, she'd been heavily camouflaged since the days when we shared the same bedroom. In her natural state old Pet would never strike you as particularly short on the hormones, but the way the film chaps had got her up she looked like an endocrinologist's benefit night.

'She's still feeling sick,' said Mother.

'Mum, I'm not. I told you I'm not.'

'Yes, you are. It was just the same when we went on the coach to Hastings. You're always sick for hours afterwards.'

'Perhaps you will permit me to prescribe, Mrs Madder – or Mrs Bancroft, rather.' I took charge of the situation. 'If you'll run down to the chemist's with this, they'll concoct it on the spot.'

'What's wrong with the hall porter, may I ask?'

'Better go yourself to see they make it up properly. These French pharmacists, you know.'

Mum hesitated a moment, but seeming to think it safe because I was the doctor, left the pair of us alone.

'Gaston, it's divine to see you again.' Petunia held out her arms. 'But what on earth are you giving me to take?'

'Bicarbonate of soda, which you could get from the chef, I just wanted a moment to find how the transformation had taken place.'

She laughed. 'Of course, I haven't seen you since that place up north - what's it called? Mother was furious. She'd no idea I'd met you, though. Wanted to hear what I'd been up to, fog or no fog. You know what she's like.'

'I'm beginning to find out.'

'She almost threw me out of the house. I was terribly hurt. After all, nothing in the slightest immoral happened there at all.'

'Quite,' I said.

'She told me to get a respectable job — usherette, nursemaid, secretary, or something. I was awfully upset, because I never really wanted to leave the stage. Not even if I hadn't half a chance of reaching the top.'

'You seem to have disproved that one, anyway.'

'Oh, being an actress isn't much to do with all this.' Pet picked at the bed-cover. 'It's the other things that count. I wanted a mink coat.'

'And what girl doesn't?'

'I mean, to get a start you have to wear the right clothes. Appear in the right places. Meet the right people. The only people I met were as broke as I was, which I knew for a fact because I tried to borrow money from all of them.'

'I know the feeling.'

Petunia smoothed back her new red hair.

'The very day after the fog I went to Shaftesbury Avenue to see my agent, and as usual he said, "Sorry, darling, nothing at the moment. 'Unless you happen to be a distressed gentlewoman."

'I asked why, and he told me Monica Fairchild had just been in. You know who *she* is, Gaston?'

'I certainly do. I was her doctor for a bit. Before she had the baby.'

'Whoever her doctor is now told her to get away from it all and have a rest. She was leaving the baby with her husband and taking a Mediterranean cruise, and wanted this distressed gentlewoman as her secretary – expenses paid, no other dibs, of course.'

I remembered Miss Fairchild was as open-handed as a dyspeptic tax-collector.

'When I got out into Shaftesbury Avenue again,' Petunia continued, as I took her hand in a professional sort of clasp, 'it struck me – wham! If I could play a doctor's wife in a fog, why couldn't I play a distressed gentlewoman on a cruise? And if I got friendly with Fairchild, there's no knowing how she'd help me along. Anyway, I'd have four square meals a day, and perhaps a bit of fun. Also, I could get away from Mum for a bit. So I put on my old tweed skirt and went round to her flat in Mount Street and got the job. She didn't know me from Eve, of course.'

'You then developed one of these famous shipboard friendships with the Fairchild,' I suggested, 'and that's how you got on all the magazine covers?'

'Not on your life. In fact, when I see her again, she'll probably tear my hair out to stuff her pillow with.'

I looked surprised.

'We went down to the ship with enough luggage for a circus,' Petunia went on. 'You can't imagine the fuss, with the photographers, flowers, and all the sailors trying to get her autograph. Nobody took any notice of me, of course, especially in my old tweed skirt.

'If I didn't know I was dogsbody there and then, I soon found out. It was "Miss Bancroft, tell the Captain I must have my special diet," and "Miss Bancroft, complain the water's too hard for my complexion," and "Miss Bancroft, if they don't stop that awful siren thing this very minute, I shall positively have hysterics." I should have gone crackers if the old hag hadn't been sea-sick. You know she usually looks like a combined operation by Dior and Elizabeth Arden? Lying on her hunk groaning under an ice-bag, she reminded me of one of my touring landladies when the rent was overdue. I think it gave me a hit of confidence.'

'Great leveller, the nausea,' I agreed.

'In fact, it gave mc enough confidence to put on my new dress. I'd brought it with all the money I had left in the world. It was the one I wore on the cover of last month's *Gentlemen's Relish.'*

I remembered it was a thing fitting Petunia as closely as her epidermis, to which it gave way for large areas about the upper thorax.

'It was the first night we had dinner at the Captain's table. He was ever so nice. Kept leaning over to pass me the butter and things with his own hands, He didn't take half as much notice of Fairchild, sitting there in her best mink. She was furious, of course. Developed a headache and disappeared to her cabin, and next morning the steward told me. I'd been shifted to another table. It was behind a pillar thing in the corner, with five commercial travellers from Birmingham.'

'A bit of a come-down,' I sympathized. 'Eating below the old salt's salt.'

'Can't blame Fairchild, I suppose. Even off-stage a star has to keep in the limelight. And don't I know it now.'

'But I don't quite follow how this made you into Melody Madder.' I felt puzzled. 'All Fairchild did was chase you about enough to have made all Cleopatra's slaves give notice.

'*That* all started when we got to Naples. When Count Longrandesi came aboard.'

'What, the terribly rich chap, who takes horses all round the world to jump on them over bits of wood?'

Petunia nodded. 'By then Fairchild had found I was in the profession. She wasn't so easy to fool as that little fat man up north. I had to read scripts to her in the afternoons, and one day she turned on me and said, "You've been on the stage, Miss Bancroft." I said yes. "You came to me under false pretences," she said. I told her an actress could still be a gentlewoman, and I happened to be a distressed one. That turned her nasty, and she made me do all her laundry. Pretty grubby, some of it was, too.

'Anyway, the Count appeared with his horses for London. He was all big eyes and kiss your hand, and, of course, Fairchild was after him.'

'Out for the Count, in fact,' I laughed.

'He saw me first,' Petunia continued, not seeming to see the joke. 'I had that dress on. Ever so sweet he was, what with buying me a Green Chartreuse in the Veranda Café. Though I suppose I should have known better than putting Fairchild's nose out of joint all over again. The next morning she told me I wasn't to wear my dress any more.'

'What a bitch in the manger!'

'After that the Count didn't take much notice of me, not in my old tweed skirt. But at least he kept Fairchild quiet for the rest of the cruise. She hardly spoke to me until we were nearly home again. Then, just before we got in she said, "Miss Bancroft, I'm sorry if I've been overwrought during the cruise. My nerves, you know. Do tell me if there's anything I can do in London to help you, though, of course, I'm going to Hollywood in a couple of weeks for the next two years. Just look at this lovely blue mink the Count's given me," she said. "He was bringing it to London for his sister, but he'll buy her another one at Bradley's. Isn't he sweet?" she said.

' "Do be a darling," she said, "and slip it over your shoulders when we go through Customs. They'd charge me the absolute earth if I tried to bring two minks through the barrier. And I can't possibly afford to throw my money away on stupid things like duty. Why, it quite suits you," she said.'

'And you agreed, Pet?'

'Didn't have much choice. Actually, the Customs' man was an absolute darling, though I suppose he rather liked the idea of running his hands through Monica Fairchild's underwear. As soon as he'd done that little squiggle with his chalk and left us, Fairchild said, "Thank you, Miss Bancroft."

'So I said, "Thank you for what?"'

'And she said, "For wearing my mink, of course."'

'So I said, "Your mink? But my dear, this is *my* mink."

"Don't be an idiot, Miss Bancroft" she said. "You know perfectly well I only asked you to wear it through Customs."

' "Did you ?" I said. 'I can't remember. Perhaps we'd better call back that nice Customs' man and see if he does?"

"Miss Bancroft ! Petunia ! You wouldn't – !"

' "As you know yourself, Monica dear," I told her, "the road to success is strewn with unfortunate accidents. Goodbye, and thank you for a lovely trip. By the way, I noticed on that little card thing that the penalties for even suspected smuggling include long periods in the clink."

'So there I was Gaston – loose in London with a blue mink cape and an old tweed skirt. I suppose I wasn't very honest, really, but I promise I'll send it back once she's home from Hollywood.'

'Jolly quick thinking, if you ask me,' I said admiringly. I suddenly felt that Pet had a bit more power under the bonnet than I'd imagined. 'It's about the most innocent way I've heard of a girl getting a mink coat, anyway.'

'After that, all the breaks seemed to come at once. My agent took me to lunch – in the mink, of course. We met Adam Stringfellow. He's a director, who was casting some models for a picture. He gave me a few days at the studio, and since then everything sort of built up.'

'And what's it like?' I asked.

'Bloody hard work,' said Petunia.

I looked surprised, having gathered from the newspapers that all she did was drive about in big fat cars with big fat chaps and draw a big fat salary.

'Do you know what time I get up in the morning? Before my milkman. I have to be at the studio by six, if you please, for hair-do and make-up. You can't imagine how ghastly it is playing a passionate love scene before breakfast, lying on a bed and remembering to keep one foot on the ground to make it all right for the censor.'

'Like billiards,' I observed.

'And I'm not myself any more.'

'Oh, come. Perfect health, I assure you.'

'I mean I'm Melody Madder Limited. With a board of directors, and things. Everyone does it because of the tax. And, of course, there's Mum.'

'Ah, yes, Mum.'

'Then there's another thing...' She looked up at me, fluttering her brand-new eyelashes. 'Gaston, my sweet – do you remember how once you loved me?'

'Only too well, Pet my dear.'

I was still getting a bit of rheumatism in the shoulder, the long-term after-effects of Clem's Caff.

'Do you know, I believe you're the only friend I've left in the world? And I need help, darling.'

'Good Lord, do you?'

'Desperately. I'm in terrible trouble.'

'Oh, yes?'

I looked cagey, knowing the sort of trouble girls specially reserve the doctors among their old friends for. But Petunia went on:

'It's all Mum's fault, really. Promise cross your heart you won't say a word?'

'Of course not. We doctors, you know. Professional secrecy.'

'Well, I'll tell you. It's simply that – '

But at that moment Mum arrived back with the medicine.

'This will have your daughter spry in no time,' I told her, shaking the bottle. 'I particularly hope she's in form again tomorrow night, because I've been asked to invite her to Lord Nutbeam's little party.'

'She'll have to get permission from Sir Theodore first,' said Mother. 'And from Mr Stringfellow, of course.'

'I have to ask their permission for everything,' Petunia apologized from the bed.

'And my permission, I might say,' added Mrs Bancroft. 'I'm still your mother, you know.'

'Yes, Mum,' said Petunia.

16

'I do so hope the young lady is free,' agreed Lord Nutbeam, when I arrived at his suite to explain the snags. 'I'd planned such a splendid little evening. There will be champagne, of course, and a band to play South American dances. Have you heard of the rumba, Doctor? It does my hip tremendous good. I wanted fireworks as well, but Ethel seems most disinclined.'

I made a consoling remark about Guy Fawkes coming but once a year, and he gave a sigh and went on, 'Don't you think, Doctor, that people are becoming such spoilsports these days? Not Ethel, of course. The dear girl is most understanding. I wanted to buy a tank of those tiny fishes in the Aquarium and serve them frozen in the water-ice tomorrow night. It would have been such a capital lark. But the hotel management wouldn't hear of it.'

I shot the old boy a glance. I'd wondered more than once since arriving at Monte Carlo whether his wife's diagnosis of pre-senile dementia wasn't correct. I supposed it was all right to make your medical adviser an apple-pie bed, and to stick a champagne bucket on his bedroom door to dowse him with ice-cold water on retiring. Or even to bust in with shouts of 'Fire!' when he's enjoying an early night, and have him looking pretty stupid running into the hall in his pyjamas with everyone else in tails and tiaras moving off to the opera. All right when your adviser's a chap like me, perhaps, but if Lord Nutbeam really had summoned the President of the Royal College of Physicians the little episodes might not have ended with such hearty laughter all round.

'But we shall have a lot of fun,' his Lordship went on. 'I'm arranging for a life-size statue of Miss Madder in ice-cream, and we can eat her. Also, the delightful gentleman from South America has promised to let me conduct the band all evening if I want. I'm sure everything will be very jolly.'

By then I was as keen as old Nutbeam for Petunia to get clearance all round and come to the party. As Pet Bancroft she'd always been a very decent sort, whom you didn't mind introducing to your friends when she wasn't in her waiter-biting mood, but dancing round the room with Melody Madder I felt could make you seem no end of a chap. The odd thing was, though I hadn't been keen on marrying Petunia Bancroft I wouldn't at all have minded Melody Madder. I supposed Freud was right – if adult happiness comes from fulfilling the longings of childhood I'd always wanted to marry a film star, along with opening for England at Lord's and beating the school record of twenty-four strawberry ices at a sitting. The only snag was not much liking the idea of getting into bed every night with a limited company.

I idled away the following day seeing some of the films, which were all about peasants and chaps in factories who took a gloomy view of life, then I put on my white dinner-jacket and wandered into Lord Nutbeam's party. Sure enough, there was Petunia, bursting at the gussets with bewitchery.

'Miss Madder.' I bowed. 'May I have the pleasure of this dance?'

'Gaston, darling ! But I must introduce you to Sir Theodore first.'

I'd heard of the chief financial wizard of Union Jack Films, of course, generally making speeches after eight-course banquets saying how broke he was.

'What's he like?' I asked.

'Oh, perfectly easy and affable, As long as you're used to dealing with the commissars in charge of Siberian salt mines.'

I found him sitting over a glass of orange juice, with the expression of an orang-outang suffering from some irritating skin disease.

'Of course you know Quinny Finn?'

Of course, everyone knew Quintin Finn. You keep seeing him on the pictures, dressed in a duffel coat saying such things as Up Periscope, Bombs Gone, or Come On Chaps, Let's Dodge It Through The Minefield. Actually, he was a little weedy fellow, who smelt of perfume.

'And this is Adam Stringfellow.'

I'd always imagined film directors were noisy chaps with large cigars, but this was a tall, gloomy bird with a beard, resembling those portraits of Thomas Carlyle.

Everyone shook hands very civilly and I felt pretty pleased with myself, particularly with my old weakness for the theatre. I was wondering if Pet perhaps retained the passions of Porterhampton, when she interrupted my thoughts with:

'I'd particularly like you to meet Mr Hosegood.'

Petunia indicated the fattest little man I'd seen outside the obesity clinic. He had a bald head, a moustache like a squashed beetle, and a waist which, like the Equator, was a purely imaginary line equidistant from the two poles.

'My future husband,' ended Petunia. 'Shall we dance, Gaston?'

I almost staggered on to the floor. It was shock enough finding Petunia already engaged. But the prospect of such a decent sort of girl becoming shackled for life to this metabolic monstrosity struck me as not only tragic but outrageously wasteful.

'Congratulations,' I said.

'Congratulations? What about?'

'Your engagement.'

'Oh, yes. Thanks. It's supposed to be a secret. Studio publicity want to link me with Quinny Finn.'

'I hope you'll be very happy.'

'Thanks.'

'I'll send a set of coffee-spoons for the wedding.'

'Thanks.'

We avoided Lord Nutbeam, chasing some Italian actress with a squeaker.

'Gaston – ' began Petunia,

'Yes?'

'That's exactly what I wanted to talk to you about yesterday. Jimmy Hosegood, I mean. I don't want to marry him at all.'

'You don't?' I looked relieved. 'That's simple, then. Just tell the chap.'

'But Sir Theodore and Mum want me to.'

'Well, tell them, then.'

'You try telling them.'

I could see her point.

'Gaston, I need your help. Terribly. Don't you see, I've simply no one else in the world to turn to? How on earth can I get rid of Jimmy?'

I danced round in silence. It seemed a case of Good Old Grimsdyke again always tackling other people's troubles, helping them to get out of engagements or into St Swithin's.

'This chap Hosegood's in the film business?'

She shook her head. 'He's in gowns. He's got lots of factories in Manchester somewhere. But he puts up the money for the films. You follow?'

'But I don't even know the fellow,' I protested. 'And you simply can't go up to a perfect stranger and tell him his fiancée hates the sight of his face.'

'Come down to our tent on the beach and have a get-together. I'm sure you'll think of something absolutely brilliant, darling. You always do. Promise?'

But before I could make a reply, Mrs Bancroft was elbowing through the crowd.

'Petunia – time for bed.'

'Yes, Mum.'

'Here, I say!' I exclaimed. 'Dash it! It's barely midnight.'

'The only advice I require from you is on medical matters, young man. Up you go, Petunia. Don't forget your skin-food on the dressing-table.'

'No, Mum.'

'Or to say good night to Sir Theodore.'

'Yes, Mum.'

'And Adam Stringfellow.'

'Yes, Mum. Good night, Gaston.'

They left me in the middle of the dance floor, feeling pretty cross. I'd been looking forward to a jolly little party with Britain's biggest sex symbol, and here she was pushed off to bed like a schoolgirl on holiday. I stared round, wondering what to do with the rest of the evening. As I didn't seem to know anybody, and Lord Nutbeam was starting to throw Charlotte Russe into the chandeliers, I thought I might as well go up to bed, too.

'Excuse me,' said a voice behind me.

I turned to find a tall blonde with a long cigarette-holder and one of those charm bracelets which make women sound like passing goods trains whenever they reach for a drink.

'You're Dr Grimsdyke, aren't you?'

'Quite correct.'

'Known Melody Madder long?'

'Years and years,' I returned pretty shortly. 'Almost at school together, in fact.'

'Really? How very interesting. Don't you think it's stuffy in here? Shall we go outside for a drink?' She took my arm. 'You can tell me the story of your life in the moonlight.'

'I don't really think you'd be very interested.'

'But I'm sure I'll be very interested indeed, Doctor.' She made for the terrace. 'Let's sit in the orangery, where we'll not be disturbed.'

I didn't see Petunia for the next twenty-four hours, Lord Nutbeam being in such a state after the party we had to spend a quiet day motoring in the mountains. In the end, I'd passed a pleasant little evening with the blonde, who's name turned out to be Dawn something and was one of those sympathetic listeners who make such good hospital almoners and barmaids. After a few glasses of champagne she'd got me telling her all my troubles, including Miles and trying to write a book, though I kept pretty quiet about Petunia and Jimmy Hosegood.

I'd already decided it was as dangerous to go mucking about gaily in people's love affair's as to go mucking about gaily in their abdomens, and to let poor old Pet manage this amorous Tweedledum herself. I supposed I could have told him she was married already with a couple of kids in Dr Barnardo's. I could have said she ground her teeth all night in bed. I could have challenged him to a duel, when at least I'd have stood the best chance of scoring a hit. But these ideas all struck me as leading to unwanted complications.

It was a couple of mornings later when I wandered down to the beach to find Petunia, and discovered Hosegood in the tent alone, on a deck-chair that looked as unsafe as a birdcage under a steam-roller.

'Nice day,' he said, as I appeared. 'Great stuff for toning up the system, a bit of sunshine.'

As he was fully dressed except for his boots and socks, I supposed he was drawing up the beneficial ultra-violet rays through his feet.

'Mind if I sit down? I was looking for Miss Madder.'

'Make yourself comfortable, lad. She was called on some photographing lark somewhere.'

He seemed very civil, so I took the next chair.

'Enjoying all the fun of the Festival?' I asked.

Hosegood sighed.

'I'd be happier on the sands at Morecambe, I would, straight. I don't hold with all this flummery-flannery myself, though there's plenty as does. Not that I'm one to interfere with anybody's enjoyment, as long as it's decent.'

'I expect you're a pretty knowledgeable chap about films?' I went on, trying to work up some sort of conversation.

'Me? Don't be daft, lad. I never go to the pictures, unless I can't help it.'

He sat for some time staring at his bunions. There didn't seem much else to talk about.

'What's your line of country?' he asked.

'I'm a doctor.'

'You are, by gum?' He almost rolled off the deck-chair. 'Just the feller I'm looking for.'

'Delighted to be of assistance,' I said politely.

'Tell me, Doctor – how can I get some of this blessed weight off?'

'Losing weight is perfectly simple,' I replied.

'Is it?' He brightened up a bit. 'Then what do I do, Doctor?'

'Eat less.'

'But I don't eat enough to keep a bird alive! Not fattening foods, at any rate. Nothing like – well, oysters, for instance.'

'One dozen oysters.' I disillusioned him, 'have only the food value of a lightly-boiled egg.'

'Go on? But I thought… I can be frank with you, of course, Doctor? Now that I'm getting married – Melody and me, y'know – and none of us are getting any younger, perhaps a few oysters…'

I disillusioned him about that one, too.

'How about massage?' he asked hopefully. 'Isn't that good for taking off weight?'

'Excellent,' I told him. 'For the masseuse.'

Hosegood looked gloomily at the agreeable combination of blue sea and girls in bikinis frolicking in the sunshine. I recalled a dietetic lecture at St Swithin's, when a professor resembling an articulated meat-skewer explained how he lived on a diet of crushed soya beans, while Sir Lancelot Spratt, who held that no gentleman ever dined off less than four courses, suffered violent trembling attacks and had to be taken out.

'They say in the papers it's dangerous to be fat,' Hosegood added sombrely.

'The commonest instruments of suicide,' I agreed, 'have rightly been described as a knife and fork.'

'But I've led a good, clean life. There's some I've seen in the club eating like steam shovels, and never putting on an ounce. I've only to look twice at the menu myself, and I'm letting out all my trousers again.'

'One of the nastier jokes of Nature,' I sympathized. 'It's all a matter of the appetite-regulating centre, nuzzling in the cranium between your pituitary gland and our sub-conscious fixations about Mother.

'Then perhaps you can suggest some sort of diet, Doctor?'

'As a matter of fact I can.'

Usually I prefer professional incognito in social surroundings, what with people keeping coming up and telling you all about their ruddy prolapsed kidneys, but old Hosegood struck me as a very decent sort, and even a good bridegroom for a girl preparing to risk getting stuck in the door of the church.

'The St Swithin's Hospital Diet,' I explained, producing the card from my wallet. 'All perfectly simple, as long as you remember to treat potatoes and puddings like deadly nightshade.'

'No fish and chips?'

'Nor alcohol.'

'I'm rather fond of a drop of beer.'

'So am I. That's the bitter pill.'

But he didn't seem in the mood for joking and pocketed the card in silence.

'Thank you, Doctor. I'll give it a go at lunch-time. I'm having a bite with Stringfellow in the Café de Paris. I suppose he wants to talk me into more brass for Melody's picture.'

'Talking of Miss Madder,' I went on, 'I certainly wouldn't contemplate marriage until you've lost a couple of stone.'

He looked alarmed. 'You really think so?'

'Without a doubt. Most dangerous.'

This wasn't strictly correct professionally, though I remembered a fat chap brought into St Swithin's orthopaedic department on his honeymoon with a dislocated shoulder when the bed broke.

'Besides,' I went on, 'there's always the risk of –'

I was aware of Lady Nutbeam standing in front of us, looking flustered.

'Doctor! There you are. I've been looking simply everywhere. We have to go back to England at once. This very afternoon.'

'Good Lord, really? Nothing serious, I hope?'

'My husband –'

'He hasn't fractured his other hip?'

'No, no! It's the hotel management. The white mice he let loose at breakfast.'

'Oh, I see.'

'I'd like you to come in the car with us, Doctor. I'm afraid Aubrey… sometimes a little trying, even for me.'

'Of course,' I said, though I'd counted on another fortnight of free drinks in the sunshine. 'If Mr Hosegood will excuse me, I'll pack at once.'

'And this telegram just arrived for you.'

'For me? I didn't think anyone knew my address.' I opened it. It said:

RETURN ENGLAND INSTANTLY WHOLE COUNTRY DISGUSTED BY YOUR BEHAVIOUR.

MILES

17

'And how, pray,' started Miles, 'do you account for *that*?'

It was a few days later, and I'd gone round early to his flat to see what the fuss was about.

'Account for what? It seems like the morning paper to me. Not even today's, either.

'You fool ! Read what's on the middle page.'

'Good Lord ! ' I exclaimed. 'There's a photo of me.'

There was a headline saying MELODY'S MEN, also pictures of Quintin Finn commanding a battleship and Jimmy Hosegood laying on the beach like a jettisoned beer barrel.

I gave a laugh. 'It says, "Dr Gaston Grimsdyke. the fashionable young London physician, is also tipped at the Festival as the future Mr Madder." I wonder what gave them that idea? Lots more about me, too.'

'Good God, man ! You actually seem proud of it.'

'Well, I've never had my photograph in the papers before.'

Miles got rather excited.

'The disgrace and scandal of your being mixed up with this – this – '

'Melody Madder's a very decent type, and I won't have anyone being beastly about her.' I helped myself to a cup of his coffee. 'Anyway, you've been advising me to marry and settle down for years.'

'Not to the woman with the most advertised thorax in Britain.'

'But Miles!' interrupted Connie, dusting somewhere in the background, 'nobody believes what they read in the papers.'

'Kindly leave this discussion to us. Far from people forgetting it, I had a most uncomfortable evening of ribald jests last night at the club. As you have deliberately bruited my name abroad – '

'Me? I haven't bruited anyone's name anywhere.' I glanced again at the paper, and noticed something about my cousin, the brilliant Harley Street Surgeon. 'Oh, well, you know what reporters are for getting up a story. I suppose it was that blonde in the hotel. I should have spotted she was a journalist, but I just thought she was nosey and sporting about paying for the drinks. Mind if I have this piece of toast?'

'This happens to be my breakfast.'

'Oh, sorry.'

'And what's all this rubbish about you writing a book?' Miles began again.

'Put that in too, did she? As a matter of fact, I've just sent off the manuscript to Carboy and Plover. Jolly good advance publicity.'

'You've really written a book?' exclaimed Connie. 'How terribly clever of you.'

'May I remind you that you were not trained to waste your time scribbling penny dreadfuls? It's high time you made some contribution to the progress of medicine.'

'My best contribution to the progress of medicine, old lad, would be giving it up.'

'Not to mention your obligation to suffering humanity.'

'Suffering humanity's so overstocked with doctors there's always a few of the poor chaps on the dole,' I told him. 'And all of them probably better than me. Now look here.' I started to feel annoyed with my idiotic cousin. 'I may not have written *War and Peace*, but I'm jolly proud of my modest literary efforts. And I'm not going to have them sneered at by chaps who've never written anything except the footer reports for the school mag., and pretty terrible they were, too, if my memory serves me right.'

'You have utterly ruined my chances at St Swithin's, of course,' Miles went on, staring at me icily. 'It happens that the committee is in an extremely delicate state at the moment. Barefoot has obtained a large grant from the McKerrow Foundation, which he will use for surgical research at St Swithin's if appointed. As you know, Sir Lancelot is combing London to find funds for exactly that purpose. Now the possibility of my becoming related by marriage to a woman with – with her bosom brazened on every billboard in the country, is a stick for Sir Lancelot and every other opponent to batter my chances into nothingness.'

I reached for one of his cigarettes.

'Miles,' I said, 'I'm getting a bit fed up with all your beastly little backstairs bickering at St Swithin's. As a matter of fact, you're a selfish and self-opinionated chump, who thinks everyone in sight's got to drop what they're doing and rally round to help you get exactly whatever you want. You were just the same at school, over the jam cupboard.'

'How dare you!' exclaimed Miles. 'Damnation.' he added, as the telephone rang in time hall.

'Sorry, old girl,' I said to Connie, as he disappeared to answer it. 'Afraid I got a bit out of hand with your old man.'

'But I think you're right.' She put down the duster. 'Absolutely right. I'd hate to think of Miles getting anything except on his own merits.'

'And pretty good merits they are, I'm the first to admit.'

I took another look at the newspaper. 'I suppose he rather got my dander up about the novel,' I apologized. 'Though I expect he's right. It's a bit stupid of me giving up a nice safe profession like medicine. Safe for the doctors, at any rate.'

'Do you know what I think?' Connie sat on the chair beside me. 'Listen to me, Gaston – I've known a lot of writers and artists. Particularly before I met Miles. I suppose I've run across most of the ones who've since made a name for themselves in London. I've darned their socks and stood them meals, as often as not. And I can assure you of one thing. If you really want to write books or paint pictures, a little matter like starvation isn't going to stop you.'

'That's jolly decent of you, Connie.'

This was the first really cheering word I'd had, even from Carboy and Plover.

'Anyway,' she added. 'If you're not suited for being a doctor, you're not. And it strikes me as better to face it now instead of killing a couple of dozen people to find out.'

Miles returned.

'It was Sir Lancelot Spratt,' he announced. 'He wishes to see you in his theatre at St Swithin's as soon as you can possibly get over there.'

I was glad to leave, both Miles and myself becoming a little exhausted by the conversation. But I edged through the traffic across London feeling pretty worried about whatever Sir Lancelot had in store for me. I supposed he took the same view as Miles, and was going to choke me off for disgracing the hospital by appearing in the same newspaper column as poor Petunia. It had been great fun telling my cousin what a pompous little pustule he really was, which I'd been meaning to ever since he confiscated my private bag of doughnuts, but it seemed a bit hard if the old boys at St Swithin's could use my chumminess with Petunia to wreck his hopes of promotion. I decided it was only fair to repair what damage I could. His remarks about my literary efforts had been pretty galling, I admitted, but in this country authors are thought a pretty unproductive class, anyway.

I hadn't been back to St Swithin's for months, and it was pleasant to stroll again through the old gateway and have a word with Harry the porter about the prospects for Goodwood. I took the lift up to Sir Lancelot's theatre, thinking how frightfully young the students were getting, and waited rather nervously in the surgeons' room while he finished off a gastrectomy.

'Right, Mr Hatrick, you sew him up and be careful of that tatty bit of peritoneum,' I heard him booming. 'Nurse! My morning tea and two digestive biscuits, if you please. Ah, there you are, Grimsdyke.'

He appeared in the pair of bright-blue pyjamas he used for expressing his personality under sterile operating gowns.

'Our patient from Long Wotton seems to be making a satisfactory, if not spectacular recovery,' Sir Lancelot began.

'So it would seem, sir.'

'But I want a word with you about another matter.'

'Ah, yes, sir.'

I braced myself. At least he couldn't throw anything handy and messy at me, like he used to inside the theatre.

Sir Lancelot untied his mask.

'I believe you are acquainted with this young Miss Melody Madder?'

'You mean Miss Melody Madder the actress, sir?'

'Naturally. Your cousin buttonholed me in the Parthenon yesterday with some garbled and apologetic story on the matter. I understand there has been something in the newspapers. I only read *The Times*, of course.'

'I – er, don't really know her, sir. Merely on nodding terms.'

'Oh.'

'Just happened to pass her in a crowd, sir.'

'I see.'

'Not my type at all, sir. I don't much like mixing with those sort of people. Always avoid them, sir.'

'Indeed.'

'In fact, sir, I can confidently assure you that she wouldn't know me from Adam.'

'Then I am extremely disappointed to hear it. It happens that I particularly wish for an introduction to this young woman myself.'

'Good Lord, do you really, sir?'

Sir Lancelot started munching a digestive biscuit.

'I had hoped to prevail upon your kindness to effect it, Grimsdyke. Under the circumstances there is no reason for my detaining you any longer. I am much obliged to you for calling. Good morning.'

'One…one moment, sir. I mean to say, I know her pretty well, sir. That is, I could easily get to know her, sir.'

'What the devil *do* you mean? You are being insultingly evasive.'

'Fact is,' I confessed, 'I didn't think you'd approve of her, sir.'

'And why not, pray? I am as appreciative of success on the stage as in surgery. I have attended sufficient theatrical people to know that it comes in both professions only from exceptional talent and exceptional hard work.'

He took another swallow of his tea.

'Now listen to me. You may be aware that I am launching an appeal for funds to carry on surgical research at St Swithin's. The National Health Service, of course, doesn't run to such luxuries.'

'Miles mentioned it, sir.'

'I am arranging a meeting in the Founder's Hall at the beginning of the next academic year to initiate the campaign. You are familiar with the words of Horace, "*Si possis recte, si non, quocumque modo rem.*" No, of course you're not. It means, "Money by right means if you can, if not, by any means, money." I should much like Miss Madder to be present. She is, after all, of considerable more interest to the public than the appearance of merely the Prime Minister or Archbishop of Canterbury. And in this case beggars fortunately can be choosers. You think you can persuade her? Good. Then I leave it entirely to you.'

He brushed away the digestive crumbs.

It was perhaps the odd sensation of doing Sir Lancelot a favour which suddenly gave me another of my brilliant ideas. I felt I could now put poor old Miles right back in the running for St Swithin's.

'How much does the fund need to get it off to a good start, sir?' I asked.

'Some ten thousand pounds, I should say. You are surely not going to write a cheque, Grimsdyke?'

'No, sir, but Lord Nutbeam might.'

'Indeed?'

'It was Miles who suggested it, sir. He felt sure Lord Nutbeam would cough up for surgical research in view of his clinical history.'

Sir Lancelot stroked his beard.

'H'm. Well, if either of you can persuade him, I need hardly say that I should he delighted. Keep me informed. Now I must get on with the next case. Good day.'

'Good day, sir.'

'By the way, Grimsdyke.' Sir Lancelot paused in the doorway. 'Miss Madder.'

'Sir?'

He made vague movements in front of his thorax.

'It's all done with wires and whalebones, isn't it?'

'Oh, no, sir ! It's all living tissue.'

'Is it, by George! You must be a more enterprising young man than I imagined.'

'She was one of my patients, sir,' I explained.

Though I thought it best not to tell the old boy I'd only been treating Petunia for nausea.

18

'A fund for surgical research? I should be delighted to contribute,' said Lord Nutbeam.

'That's really terribly decent of you. You see, I was talking to Sir Lancelot the other day, and he felt that – shall we say – ten thousand pounds would make a nice shot from the starting gun.'

'My dear Doctor, I assure you I shall give the utmost that I can possibly afford. I'm so glad you drew my attention to it. And what are you doing this lovely morning? Ethel and I are continuing to explore London. Such fun, you know. We are going to the Zoo again, where I find the monkeys absolutely intriguing. Would you care to accompany us?'

'Jolly kind of you, but I've got to drive out to the Union Jack film studios.'

'Have you, indeed? I should love to visit a film studio myself. If you have a moment before you go, would you be kind enough to slip round the corner and buy me a large bag of monkey nuts?'

It was a few days later, and one of those mornings which make you think of flannels on the village green, punts dozing on the river, strawberries and cream in the garden, and all the other gentle English summer delights which compensate for the place being uninhabitable most of the winter. I was still staying with the Nutbeams in their house in Belgravia, and the previous evening I'd telephoned Petunia about Sir Lancelot's meeting.

'Come and see me at the studio tomorrow,' she'd invited. 'And, darling, what are you doing about Jimmy Hosegood?'

I didn't mention I intended to do nothing about Jimmy Hosegood, though feeling a bit of a cad, like St George pretending the fiery dragon was only something to do with the roadworks.

'And he's got so peculiar lately,' Petunia went on. 'Ever since you put him on that diet thing.'

'Peculiar how?'

'Like a centipede with corns. Ever so gloomy and grumpy and biting everyone's head off, even Sir Theodore's.'

'The sudden drop in blood-sugar is inclined to make people touchy. St Francis must have been absolutely intolerable until he got into his stride.'

'He's even being sticky about putting up the money for my picture. Adam Stringfellow's awfully upset. Not to mention Mum.'

'Perhaps I might he able to prescribe some counter therapy,' I suggested. 'See you for lunch.'

I was as curious as old Nutbeam to explore a film studio, though rather disappointed to find the buildings stuck in the middle of the Sussex countryside resembled a municipal sanitorium. There were even the same long concrete corridors inside where you could fancy you smelt the antiseptic, the only difference being the place hadn't any windows and everyone was walking about dressed up as Roman soldiers and Hawaiian dancing girls. As nobody took any notice of me and all the doors had NO ENTRY on them, I stood wondering where to go. Then Petunia appeared, in an evening gown nicely displaying her gynaecoid pelvis.

'Gaston, darling! Have you been waiting long? I've been in the rushes. Let's go down to the canteen, I've only twenty minutes before I'm due on the floor again.'

'All right for this St Swithin's lark?' I asked, after greeting her warmly.

'Oh, that. Yes, studio publicity have passed it. But what about Jimmy, Gaston? I'm absolutely at my wits' end. Honestly.'

How's he looking?' I asked.

'You can see for yourself. He's in the canteen with Mum.'

The studio canteen looked like any other works' eating-place, except that being full of actors it suggested supper at a fancy-dress dance. In the corner were Petunia's Mum and Hosegood. He brightened a little as I appeared and exclaimed, 'Doctor! Don't you notice the change in me?'

'I was just wondering who the thin chap was,' I told him, though he looked exactly the same, except for an expression like Mother Hubbard's dog.

'Rolls, sir?' asked the waitress.

'Take it away!'

Hosegood recoiled as though offered a basket of live snakes, and asked for lean meat, poultry, game, rabbit, cooked by any method without the addition of flour, breadcrumbs, or thick sauces.

'See, Doctor – I'm sticking to that diet like glue.'

'I didn't come all the way out here today to talk about your diet,' Mum interrupted, giving me a chilly look. 'Nor did I expect to discuss my business before strangers. I simply want to know why you refuse to put up the end money for Melody's film.'

'I've got to think about it,' mumbled Hosegood gloomily. 'Money's a serious business, y'know.'

'As managing director of Melody Madder Limited I demand a better explanation.'

'Look, Mrs Bancroft – once Melody and me's spliced – '

'Mum, I really – '

'Be quiet. This is nothing to do with you. I can't understand this change of attitude at all, Mr Hosegood.'

This started an argument which made a pretty miserable lunch of it, especially with Hosegood ordering cabbage, broccoli, spinach, root vegetables, not parsnips, boiled or steamed without the addition of fat. Then a thin chap with long hair appeared to tell Melody she was wanted on the set, and Mum, of course, went too, leaving me to finish off with her fiancé.

'Very difficult, Mrs Bancroft, sometimes,' he remarked.

'Why not tuck into a whacking four-course meal tonight for a treat?' I suggested. 'Things will look much rosier afterwards.'

But he only shook his head and asked for lettuce, radishes, watercress, parsley, with dressing not containing vegetable or minerals oils.

'And I,' I announced, jolly hungry from the country air, 'am going to have a slice of that nice ginger flan.'

Hosegood's jaw dropped. 'My favourite dish!'

The poor fellow salivated so much as I cut myself a large wedge and covered it with cream, I fancied he'd ruined his tie for good.

I'd just stuck my fork into the sticky ginger bit, when the waitress said I was wanted on the telephone. It was Petunia, from her dressing-room.

'Gaston, you must do *something*.' She seemed almost in tears. 'It's Mum. Now she tells me I've got to marry Jimmy next month, and Sir Theodore's to give it out to the papers tonight. What on earth am I going to do?'

'I'm terribly sorry about it, Pet,' I apologized weakly, 'but I really don't see how I can possibly – '

'But, Gaston, you *must*. Oh. God, here's Mum again. See you on the set.'

I went back to my place with the nasty feeling that I'd let down poor old Petunia. But she was an idiotic little girl to imagine I could ruffle the amorous intentions of a high-powered financial wizard like Hosegood. Besides, no scheme had occurred to me except eloping with her myself, and Miles would he chasing us all the way to Gretna, Then I noticed my plate was empty, with Jimmy Hosegood looking like a cat climbing out of an aviary.

'Good Lord!' I exclaimed. 'You didn't – ?'

'The ginger tart,' mumbled Jimmy, 'Five hundred calories. What a fool!'

'Cheer up,' I told him, after he'd repeated this continually for several minutes. 'To err is not only human, but rather fun. Anyway, we'll get some of it off with a brisk walk down the corridor to Petunia's studio.'

'Studio?' He laid a hand on his waistcoat. 'I don't know if I'm well enough to get on my feet.'

It must have been a shock to his gastric mucosa, having a dish like that slung at it after weeks of fish and soda-water. But I was more interested at what went on inside the studio than what went on inside old Hosegood, and insisted he showed me the way.

'All right, Doctor,' he said, lumbering up. 'But by gum! I do feel queer.'

I'd often wondered how they set about making a film, the only one I'd seen being on the diagnosis of skin diseases in St Swithin's out-patients', which wasn't quite the same thing. We arrived at a door marked STAGE D, and went into a dim place the size of a cathedral filled with chaps sawing up bits of wood. The studio seemed to be lined with old sacks, was decorated only with notices telling people not to smoke or drop hammers on each other's head, neither of which anyone was paying any attention to. The floor was covered with an undergrowth of cables and copses of arc-lamps, there were chaps running about girders in the roof like Hornblower's sailors in the rigging, and there were other chaps pushing trolleys from one end to the other and back again with shouts of 'Mindcherbacspliz!' On the whole, I was rather disappointed. It reminded me of the St Swithin's operating theatre — the object of attention was illuminated with bright lights, it all seemed highly disorganized to the onlooker, there was nowhere to sit and rest your feet, and everyone not working was drinking cups of tea.

In the far corner was a typical night-club, except that it had no roof and all the guests in evening dress were reading the morning paper or knitting. In the middle stood Petunia talking to Quintin Finn, and pretty smashing she looked too, with her red hair glittering in the lights. Hosegood was meanwhile complaining he wanted to sit down, and noticing a canvas chair next to the camera with MELODY MADDER stencilled on the back I eased him into it.

'Right, children,' said Adam Stringfellow, who seemed to be a sort of referee, 'we're going now. Quiet, please.'

'Quiet!' yelled the two assistant directors, more young chaps with long hair who acted as linesmen.

Someone in the background went on hammering, sounding like a machine gun at a funeral.

'Quiet!' yelled all three directors. 'Ready, Melody?' asked Stringfellow. 'Take one, Action.'

Just at that moment I sneezed.

'Quiet!'

'Terribly sorry,' I apologized. 'Purely reflex action.'

'Quiet!'

'Speck of dust, I'm afraid.'

'Quiet!'

'Rather dusty places, these Studios.'

'For God's sake!' shouted Stringfellow. 'Can't you control yourself at your age? We'll go again. Stand by, everyone. Take two, Action.'

Hosegood hiccupped.

'Would you have the kindness to hiccup just a little more softly, Mr Hosegood?' asked Stringfellow. 'I fear it may inconvenience us by getting on the sound-track. Once again. Take three. Action.'

But Quintin Finn had some dandruff on his collar, and a chap with a whisk came to brush it off.

'Take four,' continued Stringfellow, now looking like Thomas Carlyle in the middle of one of his famous attacks of the sulks. 'This is only costing us a hundred and fifty quid a minute. All right. Melody? Action.'

'One second,' said Petunia's mum.

'Oh, God,' said Stringfellow.

'My daughter's hair's not right at the back.'

I began to feel sorry for the Stringfellow chap, even though he didn't understand the elements of nasal physiology.

'Make-up! Please fix Miss Madder's hair. At the back.'

They got ready to start again, and I was feeling pretty excited at seeing a real film being shot, when there was a shout from the back of 'Tea break!' and everyone knocked off for a cup and a bun.

I didn't have the chance for a word with Melody, because she was kept talking in a corner by Adam Stringfellow. And anyway my attention was divided between Hosegood, who'd gone green, and Quintin Finn, who was asking my opinion of all his pictures.

'Do go and see my next one, dear,' said Quintin. 'I'm a commando major, and it's ever so exciting. There goes the shooting bell again. I *do* so hope this won't make us late this evening. My chauffeur Roland gets ever so cross if I keep him waiting, the naughty thing.'

'With the permission of Mrs Madder and the man with the chronic hay-fever,' Stringfellow announced, as the bell stopped, 'we will now go again. Quiet everyone, for God's sake. At your marks, Melody? Right. Take five. Action.'

That time they started, but Melody got her lines mixed up.

'Again,' said Stringfellow, with the expression of Sir Lancelot Spratt when the gastroscope bulb went out. 'No wonder people watch television. Take six. Action.'

Poor Melody, possibly rattled by the sight of Hosegood undoing his waistcoat, made a mess of it again.

'In Heaven's name, Miss Madder! You've only to say, "Thank you for a wonderful evening." Do try and concentrate, darling, *please*.'

'Don't you talk to my daughter in that tone,' said Mum.

'If you interrupt any more, Mrs Madder, I shall ask you to leave the set.'

She got up. 'You will, will you? And where would any of you be without my daughter, I'd like to know?'

'I'm sorry, Mrs Madder. Deeply sorry. But I am suffering from bad nerves and an inadequate budget and I cannot stand any more nonsense from you or anyone – '

There was a howl beside me, as Hosegood staggered to his feet gripping his epigastrium.

'Damn it!' he gasped. 'It's all the fault of that bloody ginger tart!'

'What did you call my daughter, you swine?' Mum shouted. 'Marry her? Over my dead body!'

And she hit him on the head with a convenient carpenter's hammer.

19

'What am I supposed to do at this performance, anyway?' asked Petunia.

'Nothing, except read Sir Lancelot's little speech. I've sub-edited it a bit, by the way. I didn't think there was much point in your quoting in Latin.'

'Won't I have to talk to a lot of doctors?'

'Only my cousin Miles, and he's been incapable of speech for days. The posh job he's after at St Swithin's is decided next Thursday week.'

Petunia lit a cigarette.

'One thing, I'm not half so scared of doctors and hospitals as I used to be. Not after visiting poor dear Jimmy after his accident.'

'How is the patient, by the way?'

'Oh, fine. The doctors have let him out for convalescence. He's gone to Morecambe.'

It was the middle of September and autumn had come to London, with the news-vendors' placards changing from CLOSE OF PLAY to CLASSIFIED RESULTS and the first fierce winds starting to tear the summer dresses off the trees. I'd just picked up Petunia at her Chelsea flat and was driving her across to Sir Lancelot's meeting in St Swithin's.

'I'll nip in and collect his Lordship and his lolly,' I said, drawing up in Belgrave Square. 'Once you've said your little piece he's only got to hand Sir Lancelot his ten thousand quid, then we can all go off and have a drink. It's as simple as that.'

I found Lord Nutbeam sitting by the fire, sealing the envelope.

'Hello,' I greeted him. 'And how are we feeling this morning?'

I'd become a little worried about my patient in the past few weeks. He'd been oddly subdued and gloomy, and inclined to sit staring out of the window, like in his worst Long Wotton days. But I supposed this was reasonable in a chap who'd just finished a couple of months trying out all the night-clubs in London,

'I am still a little low, thank you, Doctor. A little low. Indeed, I fear I'm hardly up to the strain of presenting my modest donation in person.'

I nodded. 'I certainly wouldn't recommend a stuffy meeting if you don't feel equal to it. Though everyone will he frightfully disappointed, of course.'

'Besides, I have a visitor calling at noon, and I shouldn't like to keep him waiting.'

'I'll give it to the Lord Mayor to hand over, then,' I suggested.

'The Lord Mayor? I'd prefer it if you'd just quickly present it yourself, Doctor.'

'Me? But dash it! I'm not nearly important enough.'

'Oh, come, my dear Doctor. I assure you that you are, in my eyes, at any rate. I shall stay here, I think, and read a book. Or perhaps I shall play a few pieces on the piano.'

'Right ho,' I agreed, anxious to be off. 'I'll tell you all the nice things they say in the vote of thanks.'

The meeting itself, like any other of Sir Lancelot's special performances inside or out of his operating theatre, was organized on a grand scale. The old Founders' Hall at St Swithin's could look pretty impressive, with all those portraits of dead surgeons glaring down at you from the walls, not to mention the scarlet robes and bunches of flowers and chaps popping about taking photographs and the television cameras. I'd been a bit worried how the consultants at St Swithin's would react to Petunia as she appeared in a dress cut down to her xiphisternum, but they seemed delighted to meet her and all bowed over her politely as they shook hands. Sir Lancelot himself greeted us very civilly, ushering us to a couple of gilt chairs in the middle of the dais, where he'd arranged the Lord Mayor and some of the most expensive blood-pressures in the City.

'I am indeed sorry to hear Lord Nutbeam is indisposed,' he remarked, 'but I need hardly say your appearance here today, Miss Madder, will attract considerable interest to our cause. May I introduce one of my junior colleagues, Mr Miles Grimsdyke? He is taking the chair.'

Sir Lancelot banged on the table.

'Your Grace, My lord Marquis, My Lords, My Lord Mayor, ladies and gentlemen,' he began, 'may I invite silence for our Chairman?'

My cousin made an efficient little speech, and if he did dwell rather on the dear old hospital and his unswerving affection and loyalty towards it, I suppose a chap has to advertise. Then the flash-bulbs went off like Brock's benefit night as Petunia got to her feet. She made an efficient little speech too, though I don't think anyone was paying much attention to what she said. Next it was my cue.

'In the regrettable absence of Lord Nutbeam,' I announced, 'I have great pleasure, as his friend as well as his doctor, in presenting this cheque for ten thousand pounds to start so worthy a fund.'

There was applause. I wondered for a second whether to give them the story of the bishop and the parrot as well, but decided against it.

'This is a very proud moment for me,' declared Sir Lancelot, taking the envelope. 'As many of you know, it is well over forty years since I first came to this hospital as a student. In that not so distant age appendicitis was still a desperate operation, tuberculosis was indeed the scourge of our civilization, and pneumonia as often as not a death warrant. It was also an age when any political gentleman trying to interfere with the affairs of our great hospital would get his fingers burnt very smartly indeed.

'With the passing years, these walls which St Swithin's men grow to venerate so deeply have remained much as for the previous two centuries. But inside them has occurred a revolution in therapy as great as during those exciting times when Lister was introducing asepsis, Pasteur founding the science of bacteriology, and John Snow first alleviating the ordeal of the patient and the frustration of the surgeon with ether anaesthesia. Much, of course, remains to be done. Many of our old hospital buildings, for example, cry for demolition to ease our lives with a little space to park our cars. But surgical research is the cause nearest the heart of many assembled in this Hall today. It is certainly nearest to my own. I am sure we all have in mind the words of the immortal Martial – "*Non est vivere, sed valere vita est*" — as I gratefully accept this gift — this most generous gift — from Lord Nutbeam to relieve our cares in that direction.'

Everybody clapped again.

I must say, I felt pretty pleased with myself, as it hardly seemed yesterday since Sir Lancelot was kicking me out of the theatre for stamping on his left foot instead of the diathermy pedal under the operating table. Particularly as he went on:

'I feel I must express in public my appreciation — the whole hospital's appreciation — of these young men, Dr Gaston Grimsdyke and his cousin Mr Miles Grimsdyke. It is through their agency that we are honoured this afternoon with the presence of such a charming and distinguished lady of the stage as Miss Melody Madder.'

There was further applause, this time more enthusiastic. Indeed,' continued Sir Lancelot, tearing open the envelope, 'it is to these -gentlemen that we are indebted for the suggestion of Lord Nutbeam's most munificent — '

He went pink all over. I glanced at him anxiously. I wondered if the poor chap was going to have some sort of fit.

'Grimsdyke!' he hissed. 'What the devil's the meaning of this?'

'Meaning of what, sir?'

'Look at that, you fool!'

Feeling a bit embarrassed, what with everyone watching and the television cameras, I took the cheque.

'Seems all right to me, sir,' I said, shifting rather from foot to foot. 'Payable to you and signed "Nutbeam." I hope you are not suggesting it can't be met?' I added, a bit dignified.

'I do not doubt that for one moment, considering that it is made out for one pound four and eightpence.'

'Good Lord, sir, so it is! But — but — dash it! I mean to say there must be some mistake — '

'Get out of this hall this instant! You rogue! You vagabond! You unspeakable idiot! Never let me look again upon your unbearable — '

'I'm sure there's some explanation — ' I was aware that an odd sort of silence had fallen on everybody.

'Get out!' roared Sir Lancelot.

'Oh, yes, sir. Right-ho, sir.'

I left the meeting in some confusion. I think it was the Lord Mayor who had enough presence of mind to jump up and start singing *God Save The Queen*.

Twenty minutes later I was throwing open Lord Nutbeam's front door, and bumped into the severe bird in striped trousers I'd last seen emerging from Nutbeam Hall. But I didn't intend to pass the time of day with him and burst into the drawing-room, where I was a bit startled to find Lady Nutbeam next to his Lordship on the sofa wearing her old nurse's uniform.

'Look here!' I began at once. 'If this is another of your stupid jokes – '

'My dear Doctor! What on earth's the matter? You look quite beside yourself.'

'I jolly well am beside myself.' I chucked the cheque at him. 'You've made an absolutely booby of myself, Sir Lancelot, and the entire staff of St Swithin's, not to mention all sorts of City nobs. I go along to this jamboree, thinking I'd got the ten thousand quid you'd promised – '

'But my dear Doctor! I feel I never promised any such sum at all.'

'But damn it! You did. I told you ten thousand was wanted to start this blasted fund, and you agreed on the nod. Don't tell me you've simply forgotten. Or perhaps you've just omitted to add the noughts?' I added a bit hopefully.

'I indeed remember perfectly well your mentioning the sum,' Lord Nutbeam continued calmly. 'But I fear I never said I would present Sir Lancelot with it all.'

'But hell! Why on earth one pound four shillings and eightpence?'

'Because, my dear Doctor,' replied Lord Nutbeam simply, 'it is all I have left.'

There was a silence.

'Oh,' I said. 'I see.'

'We wondered why everyone was making such a fuss over the presentation,' added Lady Nutbeam.

'Though I assure you, Doctor, it gives me great pleasure to present my all to such a deserving cause as surgical research.' He took his wife's hand.

'I fear I have been overspending rather of late. But Ethel and I have had a lovely summer, haven't we, my dear?'

'And now I'm going out to get a job and we can start all over again,' said Lady Nutbeam.

'The men will be coming for the cars and the furniture this afternoon. Fortunately, I still have a cottage near Nutbeam Hall, and with my books and my piano no doubt we shall be just as happy. Though I fear, Doctor, I can no longer offer you employment in my household, as much as I should like to.'

There didn't seem anything to say.

'Good-bye, my dear Doctor. And my warmest thanks.'

I put my hand in my pocket.

'I – I don't use this very much.' I said. 'I'd rather like you to have it. It might be able to help you out a little.'

I gave him back his gold cigarette case.

Miles was already in his flat when I arrived.

'Oh, Gaston!' said Connie, opening the door.

He didn't look up as I entered.

'You'd better emigrate.' he remarked quietly.

'Yes, I'd better.' I said.

20

It had been raining heavily all day. It had been raining heavily all the day before. In fact it had been raining heavily as long as I could remember, and I was beginning to get the feeling of living under water.

I looked through the window of the clinic, which was constructed largely of old petrol tins. There was the River Amazon, very muddy and full of crocodiles. Beyond were some trees. Behind were some trees, and all round were more trees. It struck me what a damn silly song it was they used to sing about the beastly things.

I wondered whenever I'd see London again. I'd had a pretty miserable week while Miles fixed me up with the oil company, mooching round saying good-bye to things I'd hardly thought twice about before, such as Nelson's Column and the swans on the Serpentine. I'd already forgotten how long I'd been in Brazil, the only newspapers coming with the weekly launch, but I supposed it was only a couple of months, That meant another four years or so before I would ever again taste a mouthful of good old London fog. I wondered if Miles had got his job. I wondered if Sir Lancelot had got his cash, I wondered who had won the November Handicap. I wondered if I were going steadily potty, and would see my old chums again only between a couple of those chaps in neat blue suits you sometimes saw lurking round St Swithin's.

My reflections were interrupted by a cry behind mine of, 'Hello, Grimalkin, old thing! How'd you like another little game of rummy?'

I turned to face Dr Janet Pebbley, my professional colleague.

'I suppose so. There doesn't seem anything else much to do for the next five years.'

'Gosh, you're funny! But I always say, there's nothing like a game of cards for passing the time. When my friend Hilda and I were doing our midder at the Femina, I always said to her, "Hilda," I said, "let's have another little game of rummy, and I bet they'll be popping like corks again all over the place before we've even had time to notice it."'

Janet Pebbley and I had arrived together to share the job of looking after the locals' bad feet and yellow fever inoculations, and she was the only Englishwoman I had to talk to. In fact, she was the only person in the whole of Brazil I had to talk to except myself, and I'd tried that a few times already. Personally, I'm generally in favour of female doctors, who these days all wear nice hair-dos and nice nylons, but Janet was one of the standard type whose psychological development became arrested somewhere about the hockey stage. She was a tall, pink-faced girl, qualified a few years before from the London Femina, who looked as if she could rearrange Stonehenge single-handed.

The trouble was, I was falling in love with her.

I suppose that psychiatrist in Wimpole Street would have explained it as a conflict between my id and my super-ego, but as far as I was concerned I knew it was a damn silly thing to do. But seeing Janet every day, I somehow had no alternative. It's like when they stick a pair of rats in a cage in the physiology laboratory. When she emerged from her tiny bungalow for breakfast every morning with a hearty cry of, 'Hello, there, Grimalkin! How's the old liver today?' I knew perfectly well I should lock myself in and tell her to call me in five years' time. But I didn't. I sat at the table, eyeing her like a hungry cat in a cheesemonger's.

'What are you going to do, Grimalkin?' she asked, when we'd finished our meal of pork and beans that evening. 'When your contract's up and you go home, I mean.'

I looked past the oil-lamp through the clinic window, where insects nobody had ever heard of before were jostling in the darkness. It was still raining, of course.

'I don't think I can see quite as far ahead as that.'

'I can. This five years will pass in a flash. An absolute flash. As I said to my friend Hilda the very day we were starting together at the Femina, time always does flash by if you will it to. You know what I'm going to do?'

'No?'

'I'll have a bit of money saved up then. We'll both have, won't we? Nothing to spend it on here except fags. First I'm going to have a jolly good tramp all over Scotland. Then I'm going to settle down in practice somewhere in the Midlands. My friend Hilda's up there, and strictly between *entre nous* she could fix an opening.' She made a little squiggle with her finger on the tablecloth. 'Two openings, if she wanted to.'

I realized I'd taken her other hand.

'Janet – '

'Yes?'

'You're jolly nice, you know.'

'Go on with you, Grimalkin.'

'But you are. Honestly. The nicest girl I can remember. Janet, I – '

But luckily the old super-ego fell like a trip-hammer.

'Yes, Grimalkin?'

'Nothing,' I said.

'You're not looking very bright tonight.'

'The heat, you know. The rain. Bit worked up.'

'How'd you like a nice game of rummy? It will help you to unwind.'

'I suppose so,' I said, though I felt the spring had bust long ago.

The next night I kissed her,

'Grimalkin!' she shrieked. 'You shouldn't!'

'But Janet, I – I love you.'

There was silence, except for the rain on the roof.

'I do. Really and truly. Cross my heart, you're the only girl in my life.'

'Oh, Grimalkin! I knew it. As soon as I set eyes on you at London Airport, I could tell you'd taken to me. I don't know what it was. Perhaps it was the sad sort of look you had. I knew you'd want someone like me to cheer you up.'

Being cheered up by Janet Pebbley was like having your back scratched with a horse-rake, and perhaps the memory of it brought down the super-ego again.

'Haven't you anything else to say?' she asked.

But I shook my head, and we had another game of rummy.

The next day she left in the launch for a week at the company's headquarters in Manaus. As I'd read all the books and damp had got into the gramophone and you can't play rummy by yourself, I spent the evenings contemplating life somewhere like Porterhampton with Janet. There would be her friend Hilda, of course. And that tramp round Scotland. But I was so ruddy lonely looking at the rain, I started counting the days till she'd come back as carefully as the months till we'd both be released. After all, she wasn't a bad sort of girl. A bit jolly at breakfast, admittedly, but I could get used to that. Her friend Hilda might be quite witty and delightful. Come to think of it, I'd always wanted to have a good look at Scotland. The British Consul in Manaus could marry us, and that would leave a whole bungalow free for playing rummy in. I started to prepare little speeches, and wonder if it would possibly be a fine day for the wedding.

Janet came back to the camp with more pork and beans and a couple of new packs of playing cards. I waited until we finished our evening meal, and when the Brazilian cook chap had cleared away the dishes said:

'Janet –'

'Yes, Grimalkin.'

'I have something I want to ask you.'

'Really, Grimalkin?'

The super-ego quivered on its bearings. The mechanism had rusted like everything else in the ruddy climate.

'Janet, we've got on pretty well these last few weeks or months or whatever they've been, haven't we?'

'Like houses on fire, Grimalkin.'

'I mean, we've managed to hit it off pretty well together.'

'You've certainly kept me entertained with all your jokes. Especially that one about the bishop and the –'

'What I mean is, I thought, in the light of experience and under the circumstances, that is, you wouldn't mind if I asked you –'

'Go on, Grimalkin.'

There was a shocking crash, indicating somebody knocking on the corrugated iron door.

'Just one moment.'

I unlatched the door. Outside was Mr Carboy, in a Homburg and holding an umbrella.

'At last!' he cried. 'I am in the presence of the master. Allow me to shake you by the hand.'

He did, scattering drops of water all over the place.

'But – but what on earth are you doing in Brazil?' I stared at him. 'I thought you were busy correcting proofs in Bloomsbury.'

'My dear fellow! Luckily I was half-way here on holiday in Nassau when the news came.'

'News? What news?'

'But haven't you heard? About your book, of course. Tremendous success, my dear chap! We've reprinted it six times already and burnt out two rotary machines. Magnificent notices – look, I've got some of them here. Union Jack have been cabling me every day for the film rights. I might tell you that Melody Madder herself is absolutely desperate for the part of the girl. Why, you've got the whole country laughing its head off with your portrait of that pompous and pig-headed little surgeon.'

This was all very confusing.

'But – but – dash it! When you gave me that contract thing to sign in London, you said the book trade was in such a state nobody read any new novels any more.'

'Ah, well, you're a doctor. You know it's sometimes better to say the patient's going to die and collect the credit, eh? Ha ha! Talking of contracts, a fellow from Potter and Webley hasn't been prowling round, has he? Nasty little man with a moustache and a dirty brief-case. Good! Well, perhaps you'd like to sign this here and now for your next six books. Substantially increased royalties, of course. How d'you do, madam.' He noticed Janet. 'So sorry to disturb your evening. But we won't be long, as we can't keep the launch waiting.'

'Launch waiting?' I felt a touch of the vertigo. ' "We," did you say? But I've got a job here. For the next five years, at any rate.'

'My dear fellow, I soon fixed that with the oil people. Your replacement's arriving tomorrow. Why, you've got receptions, television, personal appearances, and no end of work to face. Better hurry up, the plane leaves at midnight. Another few hours and you'll be facing the photographers in London.'

I wondered whether this was all hallucinations, due to the collapse of my psychological mechanisms.

'Well,' I said, 'I suppose I'd better pack.'

'Grimalkin – '

'Ah, yes?' I'd forgotten Janet.

'What was it you…you were going to ask me?'

'I was just going to ask if you'd care for another game of rummy,' I said.

Ten minutes later I was in the launch. I noticed that the rain had stopped.

21

The literary lunch at Porterhampton was a great success. I'd spent the morning autographing copies of the novel in the local bookshop, and even if most people did come up and ask if I sold postcards it had been fun signing something different from prescriptions for cough mixture. The old Wattles were all over me, and Ma Wattle even made a speech.

'We look upon Gaston Grimsdyke as one of Porterhampton's own sons,' she asserted. 'It will be a great consolation to Dr Wattle and myself, now that we have reached the later years of our lives, to remember that he once lived beneath our humble roof. But I must not keep you from our honoured guest, whom I am sure will treat us to that delightful wit which we in Porterhampton are already privileged to know so well. Meanwhile, it is my great pleasure to present him, on behalf of his former patients, with this splendid chiming clock.'

After that I told them the story of the parrot, which everyone now seemed to think funnier than ever. Though I was a hit put off half-way through noticing little Avril Atkinson eyeing me from the end of the table.

'Sorry I was so cross that foggy night,' she smiled, catching me as I dashed for my train. 'It was only the mumps, you know. Doesn't it make you feel wretched?'

'All healed, I trust?'

'Everything is healed now, Gaston. But there's just one little favour I'd like to ask you. Could you possibly get me Melody Madder's autograph? I suppose these days you actually know her, don't you?'

I reached London in time to decide comfortably which West End restaurant to try for dinner, and felt it would be rather pleasant to drop into my club for a whisky and soda. The first person I met in the morning-room was old Miles.

'My dear chap,' I said, offering him a cigar. 'How's the new job going at Swithin's?'

'Congratulations.'

'That's jolly kind of you. But I believe you very kindly gave me them shortly after the book came out.'

'Not that. I mean on becoming a member of this club.'

He seemed to have some difficulty in talking, what with grinding his teeth.

'Oh, that. Thanks. Actually, old Carboy put me up. He says an author needs a bit of standing. Care for a drink?'

'No. No thank you. I must get off to a meeting at St Swithin's.'

He turned to go.

'Gaston – '

'Yes, Miles?'

'I admit I'm finally on the consultant staff at St Swithin's. I admit I've struggled and schemed all my life to get there. I admit it is my major ambition achieved even before my middle age. But damnation! When I think of all the work, the years, the worry…and…and…you, just scribbling away on bits of paper…'

The poor chap seemed about to burst into tears, which I'm sure would never have done in the Parthenon.

'Here, steady on, old lad.'

'All right. I'll steady on. I won't say any more. Except one thing. Do you happen to know, Gaston, that you have made me the laughing-stock not only of St Swithin's but of the entire medical profession? Do you? I am aware of it. I am aware of it perfectly well. People don't come out with it, of course. Oh, no. Not now I'm a consultant. But the students…only the other day I heard one shout, "Three cheers for Clifford Standforth" as I walked in to lecture. Everyone knows as well as I do that you made the character a ghastly caricature of myself. Your own cousin, too!'

'If I may refer you to that little bit inside the fly-leaf, all characters are entirely imaginary and any resemblance – '

'Bah!' said Miles, and walked out.

'Give my love to Connie,' I called after him.

I ordered my drink and wondered if I could nip down to Cartier's before they shut and buy a wedding present for Petunia. I'd been rather startled when she'd told me at the studio the day before she was marrying Jimmy Hosegood after all.

'It was Mum, I suppose,' she explained. 'She wanted me to marry Jimmy, so I didn't. Then she didn't want me to, so I did. But I'm terribly in love with him, darling. Even Mum's becoming reconciled. Now he's got a seat on my board.'

I didn't say anything. I supposed all women are a bit potty, and actresses especially so.

'Besides,' Petunia went on, 'look at the difference in him now he's got back from Morecambe. He's even skinnier than Quinny Finn.'

The odd thing was, after Hosegood's blow on the head he could eat as much as he liked without putting on an ounce. A jolly interesting piece of clinical research, I thought, which I'd have written up for the *British Medical Journal* if they hadn't been after my address all these years over those arrears of subscription. As for Petunia, she was just the same, though I noticed she'd turned into a blonde.

I lit another cigar, and was making for the front door feeling pretty pleased with myself, when I heard a roar behind me.

'You, boy!'

I turned round.

'You, Grimsdyke. I want a word with you.'

'Ah, yes, sir.'

'Come here. And shut the door after you. I can't tolerate draughts.'

'No, sir.'

'Sit down there. Not like that, boy. You haven't got a spinal curvature, have you, from leaning all your life on the counters of four-ale bars?'

'No, sir. Sorry, sir.'

'Now just you listen to me, young feller me lad.'

Sir Lancelot sat back and placed his fingers together.

'I recall you once tried to make a fool of me as a student. Some nonsense about distributing invitations for my nonexistent birthday party. I could easily forgive that, knowing your pathetically infantile sense of humour. But I cannot forgive your making a much bigger fool of me in front of a duke, a marquis, and a couple of earls, not to mention a mixed bag of civil dignitaries. And please chuck that cigar away. If you haven't the taste to choose something better, my advice is to give up smoking.'

'Yes, sir. Terribly sorry, sir. But I did explain in my letter of apology how I'd sort of put the *carte blanche* before the horse.'

'An explanation is not an excuse. Fortunately for St Swithin's, nobody quite understood what passed between us on the platform. I suppose they were all too intent looking at the young woman you brought. Equally fortunately, Sir James McKerrow was singularly sympathetic when I confided the story – not to mention singularly amused – and donated an additional ten thousand pounds from the funds of his Foundation. None of this prevents my telling you, Grimsdyke, that you are a young man of extremely limited intelligence, mediocre ability, flabby moral fibre, and more bright ideas than are good for you. The fact that you, a grown adult, let everyone push you about as they wish is a perfect disgrace, particularly when it's your own cousin. You understand me?'

'Yes, sir. Exactly, sir.'

'You agree with me?'

'I suppose I do, sir.'

'You will kindly take pains to mend your ways in future. Please remember however much your name appears in the papers, as far as I am concerned you're still the miserable little moronic worm I remember when you first stuck your beastly acne-infected face into my operating theatre.'

'Yes, sir.'

'Good,' said Sir Lancelot, suddenly very affable. 'I thought I'd get that over to prevent yer getting a swelled head. Now let's have a drink, and I'll buy you a decent cigar.'

It was midnight when Sir Lancelot and I left the club together.

'Can I give you a lift?' he asked. 'Though I suppose you've got a Rolls of your own now.'

'I'm sticking to the old 1930 Bentley, thank you, sir.'

'And what are you going to do now?'

'Write another book for Mr Carboy, I suppose.'

'No more medicine?'

'I'm afraid not, sir.'

'It's nothing to be ashamed of. Medical truants have played as much of a part in helping our world forward as a good many doctors. And personally I find nothing so stimulating as the smell of burning boats. But you'll miss it.'

'I think perhaps I shall, really, sir.'

'However, as you will remain on the Medical Council's *Register* till death or striking off do you part, you are perfectly at liberty to open an abcess or deliver a baby whenever the occasion arises and you happen to feel like it. And you probably will. Medicine, like murder, will out.'

'Unless I send my cases to Miles at St Swithin's.' I smiled.

'If you see him, by the way, say I'm sorry I made him sweat a bit over his appointment. Of course, it was a foregone conclusion. I just wanted to cut him down to size. That, Grimsdyke, is one of the most valuable operations in the whole repertoire of surgery. Good night, my boy.'

'Good night, sir.'

'And you might also tell your cousin I knew perfectly well he didn't have a nervous breakdown at that examination. But I don't really think a fellow ought to get bottled just before he comes up for his finals.'

Sir Lancelot drove off, leaving me with plenty of food for thought. I realized more than ever what a really great chap he was. But the most important thing about him was having such a jolly good sense of humour.

RICHARD GORDON

DOCTOR IN THE HOUSE

Richard Gordon's acceptance into St Swithin's medical school came as no surprise to anyone, least of all him – after all, he had been to public school, played first XV rugby, and his father was, let's face it, 'a St Swithin's man'. Surely he was set for life. It was rather a shock then to discover that, once there, he would actually have to work, and quite hard. Fortunately for him, life proved not to be all dissection and textbooks after all… This hilarious hospital comedy is perfect reading for anyone who's ever wondered exactly what medical students get up to in their training. Just don't read it on your way to the doctor's!

'Uproarious, extremely iconoclastic' – *Evening News*
'A delightful book' – *Sunday Times*

DOCTOR AT SEA

Richard Gordon's life was moving rapidly towards middle-aged lethargy – or so he felt. Employed as an assistant in general practice – the medical equivalent of a poor curate – and having been 'persuaded' that marriage is as much an obligation for a young doctor as celibacy for a priest, he sees the rest of his life stretching before him. Losing his nerve, and desperately in need of an antidote, he instead signs on with the Fathom Steamboat Company. What follows is a hilarious tale of nautical diseases and assorted misadventures at sea. Yet he also becomes embroiled in a mystery – what is in the Captain's stomach-remedy? And, more to the point, what on earth happened to the previous doctor?

'Sheer unadulterated fun' – *Star*

RICHARD GORDON

DOCTOR AT LARGE

Dr Richard Gordon's first job after qualifying takes him to St Swithin's where he is enrolled as Junior Casualty House Surgeon. However, some rather unfortunate incidents with Mr Justice Hopwood, as well as one of his patients inexplicably coughing up nuts and bolts, mean that promotion passes him by – and goes instead to Bingham, his odious rival. After a series of disastrous interviews, Gordon cuts his losses and visits a medical employment agency. To his disappointment, all the best jobs have already been snapped up, but he could always turn to general practice...

DOCTOR GORDON'S CASEBOOK

'Well, I see no reason why anyone should expect a doctor to be on call seven days a week, twenty-four hours a day. Considering the sort of risky life your average GP leads, it's not only inhuman but simple-minded to think that a doctor could stay sober that long...'

As Dr Richard Gordon joins the ranks of such world-famous diarists as Samuel Pepys and Fanny Burney, his most intimate thoughts and confessions reveal the life of a GP to be not quite as we might expect... Hilarious, riotous and just a bit too truthful, this is Richard Gordon at his best.

Richard Gordon

Great Medical Disasters

Man's activities have been tainted by disaster ever since the serpent first approached Eve in the garden. And the world of medicine is no exception. In this outrageous and strangely informative book, Richard Gordon explores some of history's more bizarre medical disasters. He creates a catalogue of mishaps including anthrax bombs on Gruinard Island, destroying mosquitoes in Panama, and Mary the cook who, in 1904, inadvertently spread Typhoid across New York State. As the Bible so rightly says, 'He that sinneth before his maker, let him fall into the hands of the physician.'

The Private Life of Jack The Ripper

In this remarkably shrewd and witty novel, Victorian London is brought to life with a compelling authority. Richard Gordon wonderfully conveys the boisterous, often lusty panorama of life for the very poor – hard, menial work; violence; prostitution; disease. *The Private Life of Jack The Ripper* is a masterly evocation of the practice of medicine in 1888 – the year of Jack the Ripper. It is also a dark and disturbing medical mystery. Why were his victims so silent? And why was there so little blood?

'…horribly entertaining…excitement and suspense buttressed with authentic period atmosphere' – *The Daily Telegraph*

1713838R0008

Printed in Great Britain
by Amazon.co.uk, Ltd.,
Marston Gate.